"Maybe we shoul *talk about old times, Michelle,*

Lafe challenged. "As I remember, you felt more than gratitude when I held you in my arms." He ignored her gasp, and one of his eyebrows arched knowingly. "Too bad you left that night."

"It was...for the best," she stammered. "You... you didn't want me...."

"Oh, that's where you're wrong, Michelle." So many emotions were churning inside Lafe, he had to grip the doorknob to keep from going to her. "I wanted you. I wanted you from that very first day."

Michelle's eyes widened. "Then...why did you send me away?"

"Because you're not the kind of woman a man walks away from."

He jerked open the door. "And I've never been the kind of man who sticks around."

Dear Reader,

Happy Valentine's Day! We couldn't send you flowers or chocolate hearts, but here are six wonderful new stories that capture all the magic of falling in love.

Clay Rutledge is the *Father in the Middle* in this emotional story from Phyllis Halldorson. This FABULOUS FATHER needed a new nanny for his little girl. But when he hired pretty Tamara Houston, he didn't know his adopted daughter was the child she'd once given up.

Arlene James continues her heartwarming series, THIS SIDE OF HEAVEN, with *The Rogue Who Came to Stay*. When rodeo champ Griff Shaw came home to find Joan Burton and her daughter living in his house, he couldn't turn them out. But did Joan dare share a roof with this rugged rogue?

There's mischief and romance when two sisters trade places and find love in Carolyn Zane's duet SISTER SWITCH. Meet the first half of this dazzling duo this month in *Unwilling Wife*.

In Patricia Thayer's latest book, Lafe Colter has his heart set on Michelle Royer—the one woman who wants nothing to do with him! Will *The Cowboy's Courtship* end in marriage?

Rounding out the month, Geeta Kingsley brings us *Daddy's Little Girl* and Megan McAllister finds a *Family in the Making* when she moves next door to handsome Sam Armstrong and his adorable kids in a new book by Dani Criss.

Look for more great books in the coming months from favorite authors like Diana Palmer, Elizabeth August, Suzanne Carey and many more.

Happy Reading!

Anne Canadeo
Senior Editor
Silhouette Books

Please address questions and book requests to:
Silhouette Reader Service
U.S.: 3010 Walden Ave., P.O. Box 1325, Buffalo, NY 14269
Canadian: P.O. Box 609, Fort Erie, Ont. L2A 5X3

THE COWBOY'S COURTSHIP

Patricia Thayer

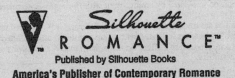

Silhouette
ROMANCE™
Published by Silhouette Books
America's Publisher of Contemporary Romance

To Steve—
My friend, my lover, my soul mate.
Thanks for always being there.
I love you

 SILHOUETTE BOOKS

ISBN 0-373-19064-6

THE COWBOY'S COURTSHIP

Copyright © 1995 by Patricia Wright

This edition published by arrangement with Harlequin Enterprises B.V.

® and TM are trademarks of Harlequin Enterprises B. V., used under license. Trademarks indicated with ® are registered in the United States Patent and Trademark Office, the Canadian Trade Marks Office and in other countries.

Printed in U.S.A.

Books by Patricia Thayer

Silhouette Romance

Just Maggie #895
Race to the Altar #1009
The Cowboy's Courtship #1064

PATRICIA THAYER

was born and raised in Indiana and now resides in Southern California. Happily married for over twenty years and having three sons, she adores the attention she gets being the only female in the house. Besides writing, she enjoys doing research almost as much, especially when it means she has to travel! Pat also loves long walks, hand-holding and quiet talks with her best friend—her husband, Steve.

Her first book, *Just Maggie*, released in '92, received second place in the Reader's Choice Awards.

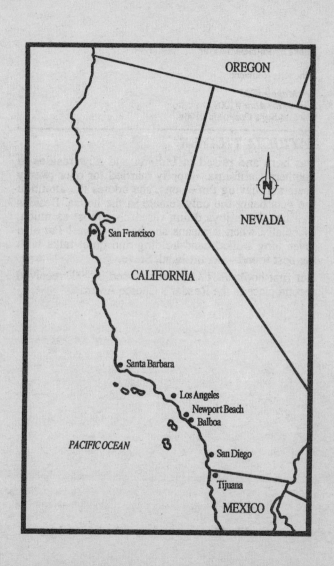

Prologue

Michelle Royer stepped outside onto the moonlit balcony and took a deep breath of the fresh, rain-washed Rocky Mountain air. A cool breeze whispered against her bare arms and caused the thin fabric of her nightgown to stir against her skin.

She leaned against the railing and listened to the restless sound of the rushing river below. It pulsated through her like the blood surging through her veins. Glancing to the left, she noticed the billowing curtains of Lafe Colter's room, their movement almost beckoning to her. Earlier that night, she'd had a taste of what it felt like to be in the man's arms, downstairs in front of the fireplace, sharing his kisses. Those kisses had ignited a flame. She craved more. She wanted him to make love to her.

Michelle wasn't thinking rationally. If she had been, she wouldn't be considering going into a man's bedroom in the middle of the night. She wanted to blame the mountain air, her glass of wine or her unbearable loneliness for acting so out of character. She knew she should go back to her room, but something was pulling her toward Lafe, toward a man who was so unlike Tom, so warm, so loving and gentle. All she cared about was being in Lafe's arms, feeling his lips on hers.

As if in a dream, she walked across the wood decking to the open sliding-glass door, pulled the sheer curtain aside and peered in. Michelle found Lafe's plaid shirt and jeans hanging on the back of a chair, his worn leather boots placed neatly underneath.

Suddenly the bathroom door opened and Lafe came into the room. Except for the towel wrapped around his waist, he was gloriously naked. He turned when he saw her standing at the door.

"Michelle, what are you doing here?"

Guided by the soft moonlight, she walked across the room. Her heart pounded loudly in her ears. "I . . . want to be with you."

"You don't know what you're saying."

"I need you," she pleaded, placing her shaky hand against his bare chest, feeling the warm beads of water from his recent shower. "And you want me."

"You're right. I want you so badly I can't think about anything else." Lafe grasped her upper arms and gently shook her. "But if you have any sense you'll turn around and head for the door. The last thing you need is to get mixed up with a guy like me."

For once in her life Michelle didn't want to be sensible. She wanted to forget the pain and loneliness of her past, if only for a little while. She raised up on her toes, her lips mere inches from his when she finally whispered, "This is where I want to be. With you—"

"No!" he interrupted, then closed his eyes as he drew a long breath, as if to regain some composure. "Look, Michelle, spending those three days with you was incredible, but . . . but it's over. You're flying back to California tomorrow. Forget me."

Her spellbound gaze searched his face. Over the past few days she had come to care for Lafe . . . deeply. "I don't think I can—"

Lafe jerked her against his body, stopping her words when his mouth took hers in a hungry kiss. Only a soft moan left her throat as Lafe's touch made her come alive. His hands moved down her back and pulled her closer to him, letting her know that he desired her. Michelle's heart soared. It had been so long since—

Suddenly he tore his mouth from hers and stepped back. She watched his chest heave as he tried to catch his breath. "Dammit! This is insane."

Michelle knew Lafe wanted her; there was no denying it. She stepped back, her hands trembling, and began undoing the tiny buttons on her nightgown. She didn't breathe as she parted the silky fabric and it gently fell off her shoulders. "It's something we both want, Lafe," she murmured, watching his face as the gown slipped down her body, exposing her breasts.

"Michelle!" he groaned. "What are you trying to do to me?"

"I think it's obvious."

Lafe released a string of expletives as he grabbed her by the arms, preventing the nightgown from traveling any farther. "Michelle, it's too soon...too soon to know what you want." The moonlight momentarily touched the tense line of his jaw. Then, to her horror, he grabbed the thin straps and pulled them upward, covering her nakedness. "I think it would be better if you went back to your own room."

Michelle's cheeks flushed. Oh, God! How could she have been so wrong . . . so stupid as to think he wanted her? That any man would want her? She felt like crying, but the past had taught her how to disguise tears. Instead, she raised her chin, turned and walked out.

It was just before dawn when Michelle carried her suitcase from the condominium, got into her rental car and drove to the airport. Her plane wasn't scheduled to leave until seven, but her work in Glenwood Springs was finished. It would be a long time before she got over the humiliation of this night.

But thank God she would never have to face Lafe Colter again.

Chapter One

Lafe Colter hated crowds almost as much as he hated being indoors. He tugged at the stiff shirt collar, momentarily relieving the stranglehold the tie had on his throat. The damn thing felt like a noose. He grimaced, taking the opportunity to swallow freely before the meeting got started. Once again he glanced around the large room, which seemed to be getting smaller by the minute as more people filed in. What he wouldn't give for a cool Rocky Mountain breeze right now.

He looked toward the back of the room every time the mahogany doors swung open and someone walked in. He wiped his palm absently across the denim fabric of his newest pair of jeans. *Is she going to be at the meeting?* he wondered.

"Looking for anyone special?"

Lafe jerked around to find Ben Stafford standing beside his chair. The CEO of Stafford Investments was a slim, distinguished-looking man. His dark hair, graying at the temples, was the only thing that gave away the fact he was over fifty.

"No," Lafe lied. "Just curious to see who I'll be working with."

Lafe had liked Ben from the first time they'd met, and their teaming up a few years back had been profitable for them both. That was one of the reasons Lafe had agreed to come to California.

Ben checked his watch. "Well, we have about ten minutes before we're scheduled to start the meeting. Would you like some coffee?"

Lafe shook his head. "I think I've had my fill of caffeine for the morning. My nerves are a little on edge and I still have to speak." Once again he scanned the packed room, suddenly feeling claustrophobic and wishing he were out at the site. *Just hang on, buddy,* he told himself. *It's the last time you have to go through this.*

The older man placed a reassuring hand on Lafe's shoulder. "A big tough cowboy like you nervous?"

"I'm also a builder, Ben," Lafe protested, knowing he had to finish this last project before he could think about going back to being just a cowboy. "And even after fifteen years in the business I'd much rather be working on a construction crew in ninety-degree heat than getting up in front of a bunch of strangers. I've always been better at showing what I can do than explaining it."

"You must be pretty good at both to be able to retire at thirty-six." Ben chuckled.

Lafe found himself grinning, too. "My retirement, as you call it, is going to be operating a hundred-thousand-acre cattle ranch."

"Well, I'll try to make this last public meeting as painless as possible," the older man promised, then grew serious. "And if Ocean Bluff is as profitable as I predict, you'll be riding off into the Colorado sunset in style. And the rest of us aren't going to do so badly, either, not to mention the jobs this project will create for the Orange County construction industry."

Lafe tugged on his collar again. "Okay, then let's get on with it."

"I plan to as soon as everyone arrives, but Chris and Michelle need to be here."

Lafe's heart began drumming in his chest. He cursed silently. Why did just hearing her name have this effect on him?

It had been a year since Michelle Royer had come to Glenwood Springs. Ben had sent her as a replacement for the project manager who had been in the hospital. Although she had only stayed in Colorado for the three days it took to finalize the project, during that time she had made him see what was missing in his life. He'd gotten a glimpse of a world that didn't consist of working long hours and endless days to fill the loneliness. Michelle was the kind of woman who could dig in deep into your heart and never let go. And he'd come close to allowing her to. She had almost made him believe that love was possible.

Lafe brought his thoughts back to the present. At first he had wanted to turn down Ben's newest project. Colter Construction had always worked exclusively in the Colorado area, where Lafe was established and had made a success of his business. But this was phase two of a project that had started in Colorado last year. Contracts had been signed long ago, before he had decided to retire. Besides, the money involved was enough that he could finish his career and be put out to pasture in style.

He smiled to himself. Oh, yes, spending the summer in California was definitely going to be worth his while.

Suddenly the door opened and Lafe blinked, then looked again as she rushed in. *Michelle!* The air seemed to catch in his chest as he struggled for a breath. He surveyed her impatiently, attempting to memorize every detail, as if she would disappear at any second.

Lafe watched her walk across the back of the room. She wore her hair differently, tied away from her face, putting more emphasis on her dark eyes. Her tailored maroon suit did nothing to hide the shapely figure he remembered. The open jacket revealed a silky cream-colored blouse that caressed the fullness of her breasts. He couldn't prevent the flood of memories that now consumed him. That night in

Glenwood Springs! She had been so beautiful, her eyes filled with desire as she had offered herself to him.

Lafe shifted in his seat. Damn! Her body was still as sexy as he'd remembered—or had tried to forget. It just didn't seem to go with the look of innocence. The look made him want to pull her into his arms and protect her from anything that would cause her harm. But she wasn't his to protect, and he might as well get used to it.

Michelle's attention was focused on a guy in his late twenties sitting in the back row. Her face lit with a warm smile. Lafe eyed the man with the sandy-colored hair and trim physique. He looked more like a surfer than a junior executive, despite his three-piece suit. The man returned Michelle's smile and patted the empty chair next to his. She quickly made her way through the crowd and sat down, and he said something that caused both to laugh. Lafe's body stiffened. Was this surfer-executive type more to her than a fellow employee?

"Are you ready to begin?" Ben asked, interrupting Lafe's thoughts. "I believe everyone is here."

"Sure," he answered, and looked over his shoulder one last time.

Ben Stafford strode to the head of the room, and the chatter drifted into silence.

"I know you're all puzzled about why I called this meeting." He gave a broad grin, and there were a few chuckles from the staff. "Well, it's to introduce the man who will be heading our next major project—developing the Ocean Bluff property."

Murmurs filled the room, and Lafe, peering through the buzzing crowd, saw the shock on Michelle's face.

Ben raised his hand to restore order. "His construction company won the bidding to build twelve one acre-parcel custom homes. And after you see the renderings and models of these 'elite' homes, I'm sure you'll agree that the completed project will exceed our most optimistic expectations," Ben announced enthusiastically. Then his expression grew serious. "You are all expected to give your fullest cooperation. This project will take top priority. An announcement will be made later this week about which of you will be directly involved. As for the general contractor—he's a stranger to many of you, but a few will remember him from our Glenwood Springs project. Well, he's agreed to leave Colorado and make Orange County his base for the next six months while he works on Ocean Bluff. It gives me great pleasure to introduce Lafe Colter.''

In stunned disbelief, Michelle Royer peered through the crowd. Her mind and body seemed numb as she stared at the man standing in the front of the room. When his eyes made contact with hers, she felt a jolt akin to an electrical shock.

She struggled to look away, but like a powerful magnet, Lafe Colter's gaze refused to release her. Seconds... minutes...hours seemed to pass before a cocky grin crossed his handsome face and he nodded to her in recognition. Embarrassed, she finally broke eye contact when several heads turned in her direction. Heat surged to her cheeks and she sank a little lower in her seat.

''Michelle—are you all right?'' Chris Lawson whispered as the room quieted and Lafe began to outline his plans for Ocean Bluff.

She glanced at Lafe again. *This is a nightmare.*

''Michelle?'' Chris repeated.

''What?'' Shaking her head, she finally turned to Chris.

''I said...are you all right? You look pale.''

She tried to compose herself. ''Of course I'm all right,'' she answered, annoyed that she was so easy to read. She returned her attention to the front of the room.

It's really Lafe, she thought desperately. She tried to listen to what he was saying, but was too distracted. The past year hadn't changed the man or her reaction to him. Dressed in a tie and jacket along with his familiar jeans, he appeared just as handsome as she remembered. The last time she'd seen him he hadn't been wearing much at all. Her heart began to race frantically. The room suddenly seemed much too warm, and she squirmed in her chair, feeling a trickle of perspiration between her breasts.

Oh, God! What was she going to do? She slowly drew air into her lungs in a futile attempt to control her rapid breathing. Why hadn't Ben told her Lafe was coming? Michelle clasped her hands tightly in her lap. Think. She needed time to think before facing Lafe. She closed her eyes. What was she going to say to the man? *Hi, remember me? I'm the woman who tried to seduce you.*

About ten minutes and several questions later, the meeting finally concluded. The board members filed up front and shook Lafe's hand, welcoming him. When Lafe finally had the chance, he glanced toward Michelle's seat, not surprised to see that it was empty.

"Lafe!" Ben's voice caught his attention and he turned to find Michelle standing at the older man's side. Lafe's pulse began to race as he moved through the crowd, but before he reached them, she turned and headed for the door. He thought about going after her, but he wasn't sure if he wanted to confront her just yet. She obviously wasn't eager to see him. Not that he blamed her.

"Lafe, come on, I'll show you your office," Ben offered.

The last thing Lafe wanted to do was go look at something he'd probably never use. He pointed toward the empty doorway. "Wasn't that Michelle Royer?"

"Yes, it was. She's expecting an important call or she would have waited around to say hello."

Lafe found he was somewhat relieved. He had conflicting emotions about Michelle. She still affected him.

"Since you two worked together in Colorado, I imagine you feel better knowing at least one person on this team."

Lafe struggled to maintain an impassive expression. "Yeah, that'll be nice."

Ben looked thoughtful. "I don't know if you're aware that when you met Michelle she was going through a pretty rough time in her life. Only six months earlier her husband, Tom, was killed in a car accident." Ben hesitated, as if he were reliving that sad time. "That was one of the reasons I sent her to Colorado. She really needed some time away."

And someone to hold her while she cried, someone to kiss away her pain, Lafe added silently, remembering all too well how wonderful the woman had felt in his arms.

"I've known Michelle since she was a young girl," Ben continued. "She's been a close friend of my daughter, Betty, for years. After they graduated high school Michelle married Tom, and we lost touch with her until I read about her husband's accident in the newspaper. It was all so tragic... she was left alone with a young son to raise." The older man shook his head. "I told her at the funeral that if there was anything I could do to just call." A proud smile split Ben's face. "Not long after that she came here and applied for a job. She's been such an asset."

"I guess losing someone you love is never easy," Lafe answered, wishing for a change of subject. The last thing he wanted to talk about was Michelle's late husband.

"No, it isn't," Ben agreed. "But... hey, we still need to check out your office so you can settle in, and then, of course, we're going out to lunch. By the way, I also have a list of people for the project-manager position, which I'd like to go over with you." Suddenly the older man's eyes lit up. "But I think I've already decided who would work out the best."

Lafe arched an eyebrow.

"She was at the top of my list anyway," Ben continued. "And since you've already worked with her... How would you feel if I gave Michelle Royer the position?"

Lafe tried to hide his surprise. He hadn't thought Ben would ever consider Michelle. "Do you think she can handle a project the size of Ocean Bluff?"

Ben didn't say anything for a moment as he studied Lafe. "Michelle's never headed a project this size before, but she's worked hard this past year. Hard enough to earn herself a promotion." He grinned. "Yes, I think Michelle and you would be perfect together."

Michelle was almost running by the time she reached her secretary, who was hard at work at the computer. "Peg, I need ten minutes without any interruptions. Please!"

The young blonde pushed her oversize glasses higher on her nose and continued her typing. "You got it, boss."

Once safely inside her office, Michelle sagged against the closed door, feeling as if she'd been kicked in the stomach. All the energy drained from her body, and she drew a deep breath trying to restore it. She glanced around the new office she'd not yet occupied a month—the plush champagne carpet, the wheat textured paper and the beautiful watercolor she had bought at the Laguna Art Festival. Her success had been won through a lot of hard work and she wasn't going to let Lafe Colter ruin everything.

Regaining her composure, Michelle pushed away from the door and crossed the room. She dropped into the high-backed leather chair behind her desk. "Damn you, Lafe Colter," she muttered. "What are you doing here?"

She'd spent a year trying to piece together her life. A year of hard work, filling up lonely hours, forcing herself to forget . . . Colorado . . . Lafe Colter . . . and what might have been the biggest mistake in her life.

She drew a long breath, struggling to calm herself, recalling the mess her life had been in a short eighteen months ago. Ben had saved her sanity by hiring her as an assistant project manager. Her job at Stafford Investments kept the creditors at bay and literally fed her and her son. Things had started to go in the right direction . . . and then Ben had sent her to Glenwood Springs last summer.

She shot out of her chair and began to pace, feeling the sudden ache in her stomach. What was she going to do? She stopped at the large picture window behind her desk and stared out at the elite Newport Beach area. This past year had been rough, but she'd made it through. Her husband had been gone eighteen months and she and T.J. were doing just fine. Closing her eyes, Michelle leaned against the cool windowpane. Just now she didn't need another encounter with Lafe that roused feelings she couldn't control.

Their first, unforgettable meeting suddenly became all too vivid in her mind. She hadn't wanted to go to Glenwood Springs, but Ben had insisted he needed her help. She had only been working at Stafford Investments a few months, and she was afraid she couldn't handle the job. Tom's death had left her feeling empty, and T.J. was having problems dealing with it, too. But somehow Ben had managed to convince her, and the next day she was on a plane to Colorado... and to Lafe.

She remembered Lafe Colter standing with his arms folded across his chest, his long legs braced apart. His green-eyed gaze had roamed over her body from head to toe. He had made it clear that he hadn't expected a woman.

"Well, you're definitely not a man," he had grumbled. "But that doesn't matter as long as you're capable of handling the job."

Michelle had been dismayed, until she'd figured out that his bark was worse than his bite. During the few days she was in Colorado, Lafe had also allowed her to see his gentler side.

Since the construction site was outside of town, it had been more practical for Michelle to stay at the completed condo that was serving as a phase one model. Lafe had been living there, but on her arrival he'd tried to insist on moving into the construction trailer temporarily. Michelle had told him not to be foolish, and insisted they share the condo.

At first Lafe had seemed distant, but not for long. Michelle found him easy to talk to, maybe because he was a good listener. She'd known from the start there was something happening between them, and she should have turned around and run all the way back to California. But, then, she had never been smart when it came to men.

Michelle's thoughts drifted off to the man who had held her, soothed her pain with his tenderness. Lafe's touch had felt too good to deny, his strong arms too comforting when she'd cried. He had brushed away her tears with his kisses....

Recalling their last night together, Michelle shut her eyes against the pain and humiliation. Her trip to Colorado had been life altering, to say the least, and had nearly destroyed what was left of her already wounded pride. After Tom's death, she'd vowed never to let another man become that important, that necessary, again. She wanted to be in control of her life in ways she had never been before. She wasn't going to fall into the same trap ever again. Then she'd met Lafe and lost her head.

A sudden knock on the door brought Michelle back to the present. "Come in," she called as she began sorting through the files on her desk.

As the door opened, she glanced up, and her hands froze around a folder. Lafe's large frame—all six feet plus of it— filled the doorway. His dark sport jacket hugged his broad shoulders. Unbuttoned, it revealed a blue oxford shirt tucked neatly into the narrow waistband of his jeans. The tie he'd worn at the meeting had already disappeared. She lowered her gaze to his pair of polished black western boots. Lafe Colter looked even better than she'd remembered.

"Hello, Michelle." Smiling, he closed the door and walked leisurely across the room to her desk.

Michelle swallowed the lump in her throat, determined not to let her discomfort show. "What are you doing here?" she asked, hoping she sounded calm and in control.

"I thought it was made clear at the meeting that I'd be working here for the next six months or so." He placed both hands on the top of the mahogany surface and leaned forward until his face was inches from hers.

"I'm aware of that," she remarked. "What I meant was what are you doing in my office?"

Michelle found her gaze locked with his. His eyes were green—a light sea green. Such a contrast to his dark tan complexion. His black wavy hair was trimmed shorter than it had been a year ago.

"Oh—why am I in your office?" As he continued to stare at her his voice softened. He seemed to have forgotten what he was going to say. Then, as though he had just snapped out of a trance, Lafe moved back from the desk, nonchalantly slipping his hands into his jeans pockets. "I just came by to say hello," he explained casually. "And to let you know we're going to be neighbors."

Michelle hated the fact that he appeared so comfortable when she had to clasp her hands together just to keep them from shaking. "Neighbors?" she repeated.

"I'm going to be occupying the office two doors down from this one. And I was wondering if you'd like to go to lunch. It's—"

"Sorry," Michelle interrupted. "I...I can't possibly go." She got up quickly and went to a file cabinet on the opposite side of the room. She needed to get as far away from him as possible. His presence seemed to fill her spacious office. She sent up a silent prayer as she pulled open a drawer. *Dear God, help me get through this!* Pulling out a file, she closed the drawer, took a deep breath and turned around to face him. "I have too much work to do."

His look told her he was unconvinced.

"Well, you have to eat. Or are you in the habit of skipping lunches?"

He made a slow, deliberate appraisal of her figure, letting her know he liked what he saw.

Michelle felt her cheeks grow warm, and her temper began to flare. "Lafe, I'm not the same...person you remember from last summer." She drew a breath. "I acted irresponsibly, but believe me I've learned from my mistake. That weekend I spent in Colorado...it's in the past and...I'd like to leave it there," she finished firmly.

Lafe raised a hand. "Michelle, really—"

"No," she interrupted, feeling her knees beginning to go weak and not knowing if it was her anger or the effect he had on her. "Let me finish."

He motioned with a sweeping hand. "Sure, be my guest."

Taking a shaky breath, she began again. "Surely you can't think you can walk in here and...and expect..." She paused, finding it difficult to put her feelings into words. "Lafe, try to understand. I was going through a rough time in my life...and I'll always be grateful for your...your friendship. But I'm not the same person you knew then."

His silent, unreadable stare unnerved her more than anything he might have said. But she couldn't lose her nerve now. He had to understand how she felt. "I know that puts us in an awkward situation," she continued, "especially since you'll be working here for the summer. I want you to know I'll do everything possible to make sure that Ocean

Bluff is a success, but ours will be a business relationship—and that's all!''

Lafe walked back to the desk. She hated his cool attitude. He seemed so sure of himself. He was silent for what seemed like an eternity, then finally he faced her.

''Nice speech, Michelle,'' he stated, his voice and face expressionless. ''I'm happy your life has turned around, and you're right, you have changed. However, I think I need to set you straight about a few things. I came here to work on the Ocean Bluff project because I am under contract. This is phase two of a deal Ben and I worked out two years ago. I'm not crazy about being in California, but I have a job to do—a big job. Believe me, I have nothing other than business in mind.''

Michelle's face reddened as she realized how presumptuous she'd been to jump to conclusions. *Great going, Royer! Let's see if you can fit your other foot in your mouth.* How much of her emotions had she revealed by protesting too much over a relationship he apparently never intended to pursue?

Lafe hadn't meant to embarrass Michelle. Hell, no! If he had his choice he'd pull her into his arms and kiss the daylights out of her.

It had been the same since the moment they'd met. He had felt a strange need to protect her that first day he'd found her wandering around his site as if she were lost, totally unaware of the surrounding dangers. If he hadn't tackled her to the ground and rolled her out of the truck's path... Hell! That near miss had taken ten years off his life.

But when he had raised his head to tell her what he thought of her foolishness all he could do was stare at the woman cradled beneath his body. She was so damn pretty it took his breath away. Her angel face was accented by large doe eyes and long chestnut hair that fanned out against the ground. A small nose turned up just a little on the end, finished off perfectly with a peppering of light brown freckles. And her body... her body could turn a man inside out. The entire time she was there in Colorado it had been hard to disguise his response.

And after seeing her today, he knew one thing for sure—he still ached for her. He'd begun to doubt that the ache would ever go away. He frowned in frustration as he caught sight of the gold framed photo next to the phone on her desk. He picked up the picture and studied it curiously. So this was Tom Royer, her husband, her lover. He could feel his body stiffen as he thought of someone else being so important to her. Suddenly he became aware of Michelle watching him, and carefully set the photo back down.

"As for lunch, I wasn't asking for a date, Michelle. Ben and a few of the staff are going to meet at the Red Onion about one o'clock for a celebration. So if you can manage to get away...you're welcome to come." He shrugged. "But if you can't, you can't." He walked to the door, knowing this wasn't how he had hoped their reunion would go. Angry with himself, he paused with his hand on the knob.

"Maybe we *should* talk about old times, Michelle. As I remember, you felt more than gratitude when I held you in my arms." He ignored her gasp, and one of his eyebrows arched knowingly. "Too bad you had to cut your visit short."

"It was best that I left." She stuttered. "Our business was completed and...and you didn't want me...."

"Oh, that's where you're wrong, Michelle." So many emotions were churning inside Lafe, he had to grip the doorknob to keep from going to her. "I wanted you. I wanted you the minute I tumbled you to the ground that first day at the site."

Her brown eyes widened. "Then...why did you send me away?"

"Because, you're not the kind of woman a man walks away from." He jerked open the door. "And I've never been the kind of man who sticks around."

Chapter Two

Michelle arrived at work before nine the following morning. She was relieved that she had made it up the elevator and to her office without running into Lafe. It was inevitable that sooner or later their paths would cross, but she still wasn't going out of her way to find him.

"But," she told herself, "I'm *not* going to sneak around to keep from seeing the man."

She knew in reality she couldn't avoid Lafe the next six months, not unless she wanted to lock herself up in her office all day and have Peggy run her errands. No! She wasn't going to let that happen. Never again was a man going to control her thoughts and her life the way her husband had.

Painful memories came flooding back. Tom Royer—good-looking, blue-eyed and blond. He was every high school girl's dream of the perfect boyfriend, and he had asked *her* to go steady. Michelle had been thrilled. She and Tom spent all their time together, but her friends started complaining about never seeing her. She'd defended the relationship by saying they were in love.

They'd ignored everyone's advice and gotten married right after graduation. About a year into their marriage she realized that Tom didn't want her to have anyone else in her life. At first he made excuses so she couldn't spend time with her friends. So they finally stopped asking her. Even her father and brothers, Pat and Joe, were a threat to Tom. Holidays were about the only time she'd seen her family unless they stopped by the house when Tom was at work.

Before Michelle knew it, her husband had had control of the money, talked her into quitting her job and found reasons why her girlfriends couldn't come around. By the time T.J. had been born, she had nearly become a prisoner in her own home.

Michelle got up and went around the front of her desk. Never again. No man was going to run her life. Her thoughts turned to Lafe, and she remembered the restless nights he had cost her. On the surface he seemed nothing like Tom, but she had too many scars not to be wary. Lafe Colter made her feel things, stirred up her emotions. He'd done it a year ago in Colorado, and once again yesterday when he'd walked back into her life. But despite what her friend Betty said, Michelle didn't need a man to make her happy. The past year and a half had proven that. Her accomplishments gave her tremendous satisfaction. That and raising T.J.

So, Mr. Colter you may be around for the next six months, but our relationship is only going to be business. Michelle began to walk the familiar path in front of her desk, trying to convince herself. *Ocean Bluff will be the only thing we have in common.*

A sudden knock on the door interrupted her train of thought. She opened it to find Lafe standing there. Unlike yesterday, he was dressed in a tan western shirt, neatly pressed, with the sleeves rolled up to expose his muscular forearms. The two buttons at the neck were undone, exposing a swirl of black hair on his chest. Gripping the doorknob tighter, she let her gaze roam to his hands, which rested on narrow hips encased in a pair of worn jeans. No one should be allowed to look that good. She raised her gaze to meet his grin, and tensed, embarrassed and angry that he knew she'd been looking him over.

"Where's your hat?" she asked flippantly, leaning against the door to keep him from coming inside her office. "I didn't think cowboys went anywhere—or did anything—without their hats."

Lafe decided to take his time answering. He liked seeing Michelle with a hungry look. It showed him she wasn't as cool as she pretended.

He raised an eyebrow and leaned toward her. "I bet, if you try real hard, Michelle, you'll remember there are quite a few things I do that don't require a hat."

Lafe stood back as Michelle gasped. Then the good part started as he watched the anger flash in her large dark eyes. She parted her full, rosy lips—surely it was to tell him what he could do with his cowboy hat. And he was ready for it; in fact, he was looking forward to a taste of her temper.

"There you two are."

Ben's voice stopped any thought of verbal sparring, and they both turned around.

"Ben..." Michelle recovered first. "Did you want to see me?"

"As a matter of fact, I need to see you both." Ben's forehead wrinkled in concentration. "It's important."

Michelle stepped aside and motioned for both men to come in. She glanced at Lafe, but he didn't seem concerned about Ben's request. He sat in a chair and crossed his booted feet at the ankles, as if he didn't have a care in the world.

Ben closed the door and also sat, while, feeling tense, Michelle leaned against the edge of her desk.

"I'm glad I caught you both together. It will make this much easier." Ben smiled at Lafe, then turned to Michelle.

"Don't look so nervous," he joked. "I'm here to relay some good news."

Michelle let out a quiet breath, but was still wondering about the reason for her boss's visit.

"I did come about your work—but only to give you a little praise and tell you how proud I am of you."

"Thank you." Michelle couldn't help blushing. She was pleased to know that Ben Stafford thought so highly of her. She'd wondered if her friendship with Betty had influenced his decision to give her a job in the first place. But she also knew that her hard work had helped her advance, and she wasn't complaining. She loved every minute of it—the challenge, excitement, being able to make a good living.

"Michelle, how would you feel about taking the job as project manager on Ocean Bluff?"

"What?" was all she could manage.

"Don't look so surprised. You've headed projects before, and I might add, you've done a wonderful job."

Ben actually felt her competent enough to head an important project like Ocean Bluff? She glanced at Lafe, but he was staring at the floor. "I've never handled anything quite this . . . complex."

Ben raised a hand to stop her protests. "I want you on this project. I feel you will do an outstanding job." He smiled charmingly. "And if the job isn't tempting enough, there's a substantial bonus when the project is completed."

Michelle's breathing almost stopped as Ben mentioned an amount. She rose and crossed the room, her head bent in concentration. She wasn't too proud to say she needed the money, but. . .she'd be working with Lafe. Very closely with Lafe.

She looked up, realizing that Ben was watching her. "What can I say?" *I want this job,* she thought as she shrugged. "You've caught me off guard with this one."

"Come on, Michelle," Ben coaxed. "It isn't like you to hedge on a challenge. We're all willing to give you the help you'll need—besides, you've worked with Lafe before." He quickly glanced at the man in the next seat, then back at her. "Look, I have a meeting in a few minutes. Why don't you think about it and get back to me by the end of the day?"

Michelle nodded and Ben walked to the door.

"Oh, Ben," she called after him, smiling, "thanks."

"I don't deserve all the thanks. You've earned it." He walked out the door.

Lafe stood and started to follow, but Michelle called after him.

"Thank you, too," she said shyly. "It was nice of you to give me this opportunity."

Lafe's dark eyes grew intense. "I'm very seldom nice when it comes to business. So you're thanking the wrong person. It was Ben's idea that you be assigned as project manager, not mine." He started to leave again, then stopped. "And I'm not sure that it's such a good idea."

Before Michelle knew what had happened, she was standing in her office alone. Maybe it was for the best, though. She needed time to think, and definitely time to cool off. How dared he talk to her like that? How dared he insinuate that she wasn't qualified for the job? How dared he!

She brushed her hair away from her face, wishing she'd taken the time this morning to tie it back. She should probably get it cut; it would be easier to take care of. Short hair seemed to be all the rage, especially with lady executives. *Oh, what was she thinking about her hair for?* Maybe it was so she wouldn't rush down the hall and strangle one cowboy contractor. "Oh, that man," she growled, folding her arms across her chest. "Why did he have to show up here?"

"What man?"

Michelle jerked around to find Chris Lawson at the door. "Oh, Chris. What do you need?" Her greeting didn't sound very inviting, and she suddenly felt guilty. He had never once turned her, or her numerous questions, away.

"I'm not sure."

"I'm sorry, Chris," she apologized, motioning for him to come in. "It's been a rough morning."

"You call getting assigned to Ocean Bluff rough?" he asked.

"You've heard already?"

"Michelle, you know our building has the best grapevine in the area. Besides, Ben talked to me yesterday," he admitted.

"Ben asked you about me?"

Chris shrugged. "He just wanted to know if I felt you were ready to handle Ocean Bluff."

"And..."

The handsome blonde tossed her the boyish grin that all the women in the office would die for. "I said absolutely."

"So you think I should take it?"

"Absolutely."

Oh, she needed the job all right. Tom had always worked, but dreamed of being his own boss. He'd tried numerous business ventures, but none of them had ever made any money. Later, Michelle found out that he had mortgaged their small stucco home to the limit a year before his fatal accident. Even after refinancing, her payments were a struggle, and the faltering real-estate market made her house worth less than what she owed. Yes, she definitely needed this job—and the bonus. But more important, she wanted the project.

The past year and a half working at Stafford Investments had been the best. For the first time in a long while, she felt great about herself. She had gained self-confidence knowing she was good at her job.

The only drawback she could see in heading this project was the fact that some men had trouble working for a woman. Did that include Lafe Colter? Would he let her do her job? She thought back to Colorado, knowing he hadn't been the easiest man to work for. But he was fair, and when it came to business, he was *total* business. And if she headed Ocean Bluff she would have to rely heavily on Lafe's cooperation.

"You're not going to let this chance slip away, are you?" Chris frowned. "I thought I taught you better than that, Michelle."

She smiled. "You taught me very well, Chris." She could tell that he really wanted her to have this opportunity. And so did she. "Thank you."

"You worked hard," he countered with a shrug. "It's time things started going your way for a change."

She suspected Chris knew something about her past, but he never overstepped the bounds of their working relationship to ask more. "They have...with a little help from my friends." It would take a long time for her to completely trust a man again, but she considered Chris a good friend.

"My pleasure. So you're going to tell Ben, yes?"

Michelle couldn't help thinking about Lafe, but the Ocean Bluff project was too important—to both of them. "You're right, I'm going to tell Ben, yes."

It was seven o'clock that evening and the building was nearly deserted, but Lafe was still hard at work at the drawing table in his temporary office. He didn't mind staying. It was his job to go over the blueprints to make sure all corrections had been made before they went for final approval. And he wanted to be at the site first thing tomorrow. If only he could keep his mind on his work.

Ever since his arrival yesterday morning his concentration had been all but nonexistent. Michelle's face always seemed to interrupt his train of thought. Tossing the pencil on the table, Lafe rose from his stool and began pacing.

"C'mon, Colter, this is crazy! You're acting like a randy teenager." He combed his hand through his hair, reminding himself that he had turned thirty-six just this past month. There had never been a job he hadn't taken on and completed to everyone's satisfaction. Women had not intruded on his work, not until now, not until a stubborn brown-eyed vixen had walked into his life a year ago. Frustrated, he shoved at his shirtsleeves, turned on the radio and forced himself to return to the drawing table.

Outside, standing in the hallway, Michelle knocked on Lafe's door, but no one answered. Bravely she turned the knob and peered into the office. He was there, all right, sitting at a drawing table with his back to her. His head was bent low, and he was totally absorbed in his work. She stepped inside and spoke his name again, but the rhythmic sound of music drowned her out. Hesitant to disturb him, Michelle thought it might be best to leave.

Instead she became preoccupied with watching the muscles across his back flex with his slightest movement. His broad shoulders had no trouble whatsoever filling out his shirt. She let her gaze follow the tapered material down his spine, taking the time to admire his slim waist. His jeans were pulled tightly over his hips and thighs as he straddled the high stool; his long legs were stretched out under the table, where his booted foot tapped to the country music.

Michelle squeezed the manila folder between her fingers, feeling her pulse race. *Pull yourself together, girl,* she admonished. She could not let this man get to her, not again. Not if she was going to be working with him. She still had a lot of doubts, especially now that she knew Lafe wasn't exactly crazy about the idea, either.

She drew a breath and quickly cleared her throat to get his attention. As though he finally sensed her presence, Lafe pivoted around.

"If I'm disturbing you I could come back another time," she offered, her hand still on the doorknob.

"No!" Lafe reached for the radio dial and lowered the music, then got off the stool to greet her. "I was just going over the blueprints, looking at the architect's changes. They can wait." He studied her closely. "What are you doing here so late?"

"Working, like you. Sometimes I get more done after office hours than I do all day long."

"What about your son?" Lafe inquired.

Michelle had forgotten she'd told Lafe about her family. Maybe more than she would have liked.

"T.J.'s fine. He's with the baby-sitter."

Lafe raised an eyebrow. "I can bet he'd rather be with his mom."

"Well, I'd rather be with my son, too. But my working is a fact of life. T.J. understands that." At least, Michelle thought, as much as a seven-year-old could comprehend when his world had been turned upside down.

"Kids don't always understand as much as we think they do," Lafe shot back.

Michelle blinked, seeing a sudden flash of sadness in Lafe's eyes. It made her want to reach out and...

Where did that come from? she wondered, realizing things were getting entirely too personal. She moved farther into the room and got to the reason for her visit. "Ben gave me this file on Ocean Bluff." She held up the folder.

"So you've decided to take the job?"

"That all depends. . . ." Michelle raised an eyebrow. "If we can work together."

"Looks like there isn't any choice," Lafe stated.

"There is always a choice. You can tell Ben that you want to work with someone else."

Lafe grinned, but it was more of smirk. "And just what would be my reason?" He suddenly turned serious. "Look, we worked together before and didn't have any problems."

We did when you started being too nice, Michelle thought. When you made me forget my world was falling apart, and when you held me in your arms and kissed away my tears. Realizing where her thoughts were headed, she drew a deep breath and pushed aside the memories.

"This time there are a new set of rules, Lafe. I won't just bring you the final set of building plans. I'll be in charge of how and where the money gets spent." She glanced away. Lafe was watching her too closely. "It. . .it will be my job to bring this project in under budget. We may be tempted to take shortcuts, but I won't use inferior materials. Seven of these parcels are already sold, and the owners have stated explicitly what they want. And rightly so, since they are paying an outrageous sum for the privilege." Seeing his jaw tense, Michelle could tell that she had hit a nerve.

"I haven't made a name for myself by cutting corners or doing inferior work. Just because Ocean Bluff will be my last job doesn't mean—"

"Last job? What do you mean last job?"

He shrugged carelessly. "It means I'm quitting the business."

"But why?" Michelle knew he wasn't that much older than she was.

"Maybe I want to enjoy life a little." He looked thoughtful. "Spend some time on my ranch."

"Oh, that sounds nice." It sure didn't sound like the Lafe she knew a year ago.

Lafe rested his hands on his hips. "So, if you can get me a list of local subcontractors, I'll do my job. Don't worry, I'll bring Ocean Bluff in on time—and on budget."

"I'll have the list on your desk by tomorrow morning."

"Good." He seemed to relax. "I think, now that we understand each other, we'll be able to work together."

Michelle wished she felt the same way. "Thanks for not talking Ben out of giving me this job."

When his green-eyed gaze locked with hers, she found she couldn't even manage to swallow. "Ben has confidence that you can do the job. Who am I to argue?" He stepped closer.

His movement triggered Michelle's self-protective instincts, and she backed away. He was a large man and took up a lot of space in the small office, not just with his size, but with his presence. She turned toward the model sitting on the table.

"I was hoping to get a look at exactly what we're building. I mean what you're building," she corrected.

"You were right the first time—your company is supplying the capital and the land. Without that I'd be out of a job. Would you like to take a look at the blueprints?"

"Yes, please."

God, she was lovely, Lafe thought as he watched her walk toward the drawing table. Although small in build, Michelle didn't lack shape. He eyed the silky powder blue blouse that showed off the fullness of her breasts. Her navy skirt gathered neatly around her tiny waist, accenting the rounded shape of her hips. He raised his gaze to her face, finding her dark eyes bright, her cheeks a little flushed. Lafe clenched his hands at his sides. He knew he could never erase the memory of what it felt like to touch her ivory skin.

He shut his eyes for a moment, telling himself he had to stop. He had to keep his mind on the project, he had to think about business, not remember what it was like to have Michelle Royer in his arms. He silenced a groan and walked toward the table. "Do you know where the site is?"

She nodded. "It's a beautiful area."

First, Michelle studied the blueprints while Lafe explained each home's floor plan. Ocean Bluff looked just like its name. The homes were a Cape Cod design, something you'd more likely find on the East Coast. The structures were going to be done completely in wood and brick.

"They're going to be beautiful. You should put a light-house on the edge of the bluff," she joked.

"I'll see what I can come up with." His gaze met hers once again, and Michelle quickly glanced back to the blue-prints.

"Your eyes still get so large when you're excited," he said in a husky tone.

Michelle's smile disappeared. Her head began to pound like crazy. "I think . . . I'd better let you get back to work." She tried to move past Lafe, but only succeeded in bumping against him. She gasped as a tingling sensation seemed to burn clear through her skin. She tried to breathe, but her lungs didn't react to her need. Her biggest mistake was lifting her head and seeing the intense look in his eyes. Some-how she managed to get past him, ignoring the call of her name. She grabbed the folder off the desk and practically ran to the door.

Finally outside the office, she leaned against the wall and closed her eyes. She chided herself on how easily she re-acted to the man. Well, somehow she was going to have to find a way to work with Lafe, she decided as she headed back to her office. That was, if she wanted to survive.

Lafe gripped the doorknob, cursing because he ached to go after her. He never chased after women, not in a long, long while. He'd been burned a few times, and knew to stay away from the flame.

He drew a deep breath, released it and walked back to his desk, reminding himself to concentrate on building Ocean Bluff. Work had always filled up his time. For the past fif-teen years it had been the only important thing in his life.

He thought back to his early years. Wanting to be on his own, he'd grown up fast and hard. At eighteen, he had bummed around on the rodeo circuit and had nursed more than one bruise or pulled muscle. At twenty-one he had started coming to his senses and had decided he wanted more out of life. That had been when he'd hired on a con-struction crew and found out he liked the work. He en-joyed working outside, building, making something per-manent, a home.

Home. The word sounded strange to Lafe. Maybe because he'd never had a place he could really call home. Growing up, his parents had never stayed in one place very long. They had either been evicted or had skipped out in the middle of the night because they couldn't come up with the rent money. Lafe had been too young to remember all the towns they'd traveled through—mostly in Texas and Oklahoma, he guessed—anywhere his mom, Rosie May, could get a waitress job in the local bar. His dad, Jack, hadn't been as eager to find employment, but when he'd managed to stay sober, he'd worked as a ranch hand, and sometimes, when he was lucky, he'd gotten a job on an oil rig. Until one day there was an accident, and his dad's drinking was blamed for another worker's death.

Rosie had finally gotten fed up with her man's problems and had taken off with Lafe even before they found out what had happened. Lafe had only been eight years old at the time, and he never knew if his dad had been sent to prison.

By the time Lafe was nine, his mom must have gotten fed up with him, as well. One day she drove their beat-up truck to a ranch in Colorado, telling Lafe to wait while she went into the house. He could still remember how pretty the ranch house looked, and how he wished he and his mom could live in a place like that.

He'd wished too hard. Before he knew what was happening, his mom had pulled him out of the truck along with his suitcase, then practically dragged him up the steps and through the front door. The inside of the house was dark and scary, and so was the old man sitting behind the large desk.

He turned out to be his dad's uncle, Ray Colter. Uncle Ray reluctantly agreed to be Lafe's guardian. The Colter ranch was going to be his new home until he turned eighteen.

"No! Mom, don't leave me here," he'd screamed as his uncle took hold of his arm. He'd fought as hard as he could to break the man's hold, only to work up tears of frustration as he watched Rosie May hurry out the door.

"Settle down, you little hellion," Ray had ordered, gripping his nephew's arms tighter. "You're here to stay whether you like it or not. So you'd better get used to the idea."

"I'm never staying here. Never! Never!" he yelled, breaking away and taking off after his mom. He was too late; she was driving off by the time he ran outside. It didn't stop him from running after her, calling out her name. He was nearly a mile from the house before he finally collapsed and his uncle found him sobbing along the side of the road.

"You'd better get used to bein' here, kid, 'cause she ain't coming back for you. Now, you can spend the next few years fighting me, or you can find a way for you and me to get along. Just do as I say, and I'll treat you fair. I'll feed you and put a roof over your head. But I won't put up with your caterwauling. So dry your eyes and get back to the house."

Lafe had stood up proudly and dusted off his clothes. With watery eyes he had looked once again down the now-dark road, feeling an awful ache in his gut. That ache had never gone away. How could she have left him? She hadn't even said goodbye.

Standing at the window in his office, Lafe fought for control. He wanted desperately to break the glass and feel the cool ocean air against his skin. Instead, he drew a long slow breath, and the practiced exercise helped him begin to relax.

Damn! What had made him think of his mother? He rubbed his hands over his face. She'd been dead for ten years. But it had been only six months since Ray Colter had died.

Lafe had worked hard for the nine years he'd lived under his uncle's care, though there had been no love lost between them. The day Lafe had turned eighteen, he'd packed his bags and taken off. So it had surprised the hell out of him when a lawyer had called and told him that his uncle had left him the ranch. The place where his mother had deserted him. The place he'd swore he'd never go back to.

Lafe looked down at the bright lights along the streets below. He sat on the edge of the window, crossing his arms over his chest. The Colter ranch, just outside Durango, Colorado, was his now. He had already visited the property several times, even gotten involved with some of the badly needed repair work on the outer buildings. He'd hired a foreman to watch over the place until he could be there more than just an occasional weekend. The thought of returning excited him more than anything had in a long time. It sure wasn't the construction business anymore. He'd planned turning over the running of the company to Jeff until he found a buyer who'd keep on his regular crew. And as soon as he finished Ocean Bluff, he was planning to live on the hundred-thousand-acre cattle ranch permanently.

A sudden sadness tore at Lafe as he thought about the big empty ranch house. A family had never been in the cards for him. With Rosie May and Jack as role models, what could he expect? His parents had never been committed to each other, let alone to their son. When his mother had run off, Lafe had just seemed to stop feeling. She'd left a permanent frozen spot in his heart no woman had been able to thaw. He'd tried once and gotten burned badly. So it was in self-defense that Lafe had developed a knack for picking women who only wanted a good time, and when it was over they both could just...move on. It was safer.

Until Michelle.

A lonely ache tugged at him as he remembered how satisfying it had been to get lost in her big brown eyes, or to be on the receiving end of one of her heart-stopping smiles. She'd been heaven to hold in his arms, all soft and womanly. Lafe felt his body begin to respond and he shifted uncomfortably, then finally stood up.

Damn! Why couldn't he just let the experience go? Michelle was not his kind of woman anyway. She had *forever* stamped all over her. Anything Lafe Colter had to offer her was temporary...nothing permanent.

Chapter Three

Michelle reached for the phone on her desk. A smile spread across her face when she heard her son's voice.

"Mom! I caught a fish. Grandpa Mike said it was probably the biggest one in the lake."

Smiling wider at her son's enthusiasm, Michelle cradled the receiver against her shoulder as she continued looking over the contractors bids on her desk. "And you caught it all by yourself?"

"Well, Grandpa helped a little," T.J. confessed. "That's 'cause the fish was so big. But Grandpa said that by next year I'll be big enough to do it all by myself."

Bless you, Dad, she offered in silent thanks. She felt guilty about not spending more time with her son. "Well, your grandfather's been fishing a long time. He would know."

Michael Donovan had been a lifesaver this past year. He'd helped her by watching T.J. when she couldn't afford to pay anyone. It was sad that it had taken Tom's death before T.J. had gotten the chance to know his grandfather.

"Yeah, he told me that he started when he was seven, too. And he used to take Uncle Pat, Uncle Joe and you with him when you were kids. Hey, Mom, how come you never told me you can fish?''

''You never asked,'' she answered. Hearing the excitement in her son's voice, she didn't feel so bad about working late. ''So you had a great time today?''

''It was neat. Can I go again?''

''That's up to Grandpa.''

''Well, then, can I spend the night at Billy's house? Aunt Betty said it was okay. Really she did.''

Michelle was sure she had. Betty Stafford Harper and her lawyer husband, Bill, had been more than generous since Tom's death, helping Michelle put her life in order, offering her legal advice. Betty had also picked up their friendship as though they hadn't been separated for the past ten years. That was the most important thing to Michelle, since Tom had managed to isolate her from everyone. She had needed a friend, someone who didn't judge her, and Betty had been a godsend.

''I'm sure she did honey.''

''You can ask Aunt Betty yourself.'' Before Michelle could protest, T.J. dropped the phone and ran off.

Michelle was tickled that her son had found a friend in Billy. T.J. had always liked to play by himself, and at school the teachers commented that he didn't join in activities easily. She knew her boy was extremely shy around other people, but it wasn't until after Tom's death that Michelle realized it wasn't a personality trait. Her husband's dominance had affected her son's life, too.

Betty came on the line. ''Hey, Donovan, what you still doing at the office? Dad working you too hard?''

Michelle couldn't help but smile. ''Well, some of us have to make a living.''

''I told you years ago to marry for money.''

''Believe me, I wish I had listened.'' Michelle felt a twinge of guilt. Her life with Tom had been far from perfect, and over the years he had managed to destroy any love she had once felt for him. Now Michelle was a little more realistic.

''There are still available men out there.''

"Not on a bet." This time Michelle laughed. "I'm satisfied with the way things are."

"Even with that good-looking Lafe Colter running around in tight jeans and cowboy boots? You'd be a fool to pass him by."

Michelle tensed, knowing she wasn't totally immune to the man, but she'd never admit that to anyone. "All I have time for is work and T.J." She hadn't exactly lied. She thought about Lafe more than she liked, and she knew that their strong attraction might lead to love and love needed trust. Michelle doubted she'd ever be able to trust a man again.

"Well, it's Friday night—quitting time. So you come home and we'll take the boys out for pizza, and discuss the situation a little more."

Michelle explained to Betty that she wanted to finish her work so she would have the weekend with her son. Betty offered to take T.J. to her house for the night and bring him home in the morning.

"I want a rain check on the pizza," Betty insisted. "We definitely need to talk about your attitude toward men."

Michelle tried to rub the stiffness from the back of her neck. She checked the clock and gasped. Seven o'clock was late enough to work, no matter what needed to be done. She closed the file and rose from the chair, stretching her arms over her head. It had been another tedious week. Long days had stretched into long evenings while Michelle had worked on bids from subcontractors and suppliers. So far no complaints, not even from Lafe. And even better, Ocean Bluff was ahead of schedule.

"Ah...that felt good," she groaned as she stretched again, and decided anything she had to do could wait until Monday. She gathered up her briefcase and purse and left the office.

Five minutes later, Michelle was walking across the parking lot to her Volkswagen. She unlocked the door to the '69 Bug, tossed her things in back and collapsed into the driver's seat. Starting the engine, she then shifted into reverse and backed out of the space. Not far down the row, she found a blue Bronco with its hood raised and Lafe Colter looking over the engine. Her first reaction was to ignore the situation—someone else would probably help him . . . eventually.

She glanced around the deserted lot. Everyone beat tracks out of there early on a Friday night.

"Why me?" She moaned, knowing she had to stop.

Reluctantly Michelle pulled up next to the truck, and got out of her car. "Need some help?"

When Lafe raised his head he didn't look happy. "Yeah, I need a mechanic. Know where I can get one?"

Michelle shrugged. "Maybe. What seems to be the problem?"

"When I turn the key, there's nothing," he explained as he ran the back of his greasy hand across his forehead, leaving a grimy smudge.

She bit her lip to keep from smiling as she caught a glimpse of the dirt on his once-white shirt. He was a mess, but it didn't take away from his masculine appeal. She watched him walk to the truck and reach inside for a rag to wipe his hands.

"What about the battery?" she asked.

He shook his head. "No, it's new—in fact, I had the whole truck overhauled before I left Colorado."

"Maybe it's just a loose wire or a bad connection?"

Lafe looked up, squinting into the setting sun. "I was checking that when you drove up."

She snapped her fingers. "I could call my brother Joe. He's a mechanic."

He waved off her suggestion. "It's too late to call anyone tonight."

"No, Joe has a twenty-four-hour towing service," Michelle assured him. "Although he probably won't be able to fix it until tomorrow."

"I guess I don't have a choice."

Michelle wished she did. She didn't need a cowboy with an attitude to finish off her week. "I'll phone him from the lobby. She had started toward her car, when Lafe called to her.

"Michelle. Do you think I could hitch a ride home with you?"

Panic raced through her as she fought the urge to get in her car and drive away. *Darn, this is not the way to keep your distance from the man.*

"I hate to ask, but as you can see I haven't many options."

Lafe at least had the decency to look humble, Michelle acknowledged. "Sure, I can give you a ride home," she said.

After making the call, Michelle returned to find that Lafe had lowered the hood and was leaning against the truck. He was dressed in his usual jeans and work boots. His shirt-sleeves were still rolled up, exposing his muscular forearms. He pushed away from his truck and walked around to the passenger side of her Bug and opened the door.

"Joe will send someone out within the hour. We'll leave your keys with the guard at the gate. Get in." She shifted into first gear.

Lafe hesitated. He didn't know if this was going to be such a good idea. As much as he wanted to spend some time with Michelle, her look told him she didn't feel the same. "Do you think I'll fit?"

"You'd better, because you don't have much choice."

Lafe tried to ignore her white-knuckled grip on the steering wheel and climbed in. He quickly grabbed the lever under the seat, releasing it to give himself a little more leg room. He adjusted his long body and fastened his safety belt. Taking a relaxing breath, he glanced around the small car. This wasn't so bad, he thought as he braced his knees against the glove compartment.

Michelle was silent as she drove toward the security gate. She spoke to the guard and explained the situation. Lafe handed over his keys and Michelle rewarded the older man with one of her smiles before driving out of the lot.

"Where are you staying?"

"Ben's house at the beach," he told her, helping to check the traffic. "Do you know where that is?"

"Yes," she answered as she accelerated onto MacArthur Boulevard.

Lafe was thrown against the back of his seat as the car jerked out into the street, barely missing oncoming traffic. Biting back his comments, he could only watch as Michelle maneuvered the faded-red VW through the crowded lanes until she was at the head of the pack. Lafe gripped the handle on the dashboard and hung on, all the time promising himself that she was going to pay for this little joyride.

Glancing quickly at Lafe, Michelle forced herself not to smile, wondering just how far she could push it. She pressed down on the accelerator, silently thanking Joe for fixing the carburetor as again the car rushed forward. Coming to the hill, she knew that her car couldn't take it fast, so she eased off the gas and moved into the slower lane. Out of the corner of her eye, she saw Lafe release his grip on the edge of the seat.

"It's a great night," Lafe said, picking up the conversation as he rolled down his window. He'd be damned if he would mention her driving. What he wanted was to stop the car and shake some sense into her.

"I love the view along this road," Michelle said.

He gave her a sideways glance. Her dark hair was blowing in the cool breeze. She looked more relaxed than he'd seen her. "Maybe you should slow down so you can enjoy it."

"I am enjoying it."

When she turned to him and smiled, Lafe felt his heart leap.

With a nod Michelle indicated the setting sun, casting diffused gold and orange lights across the water. "Southern California has the most beautiful sunsets. It's just a shame that they're because of the smog."

"It is beautiful," Lafe said in earnest, but his gaze was turned toward her, focusing on her bare legs. Her short skirt didn't cover much to begin with; now it was on the rise, and every time she pushed in the clutch the material began moving farther up her thighs. Lafe's body was already warm from the close quarters in the compact car, and the sight of her shapely legs didn't help. He rolled down his window, and let the breeze cool him off.

About fifteen minutes later, they pulled into the driveway in front of the beach house that backed up to the Pacific Ocean. Lafe got out of the car and invited Michelle inside. He insisted they needed to talk business.

Well, this would be a good time, she thought. T.J. was with Billy, and she didn't have to worry about getting home...right away. Besides, she had to put her personal feelings on hold and act like the professional she'd been working so hard to be. She opened the car door and got out as the ocean air caught her hair and whipped it across her cheek. She smiled, enjoying the feeling as she pushed the wayward strands behind her ears. The beach was not more than a hundred yards away, and she yearned to pull off her heels and panty hose and walk barefoot in the sand.

Instead Michelle followed Lafe toward the familiar Stafford cottage. He unlocked the door, then stepped aside, letting her walk in first. Adjusting her eyes to the dim light, she found things were the same, yet subtly changed. She noticed new plush, wheat-colored carpeting, a dark blue sofa and matching love seat, and the familiar childhood pictures sitting on the mantel of the stone fireplace. Along the far wall, French doors led out to the patio and small yard. There were plenty of memories of the happy summers she had spent there with Betty and her family.

To her surprise Lafe brought her a glass of wine from the kitchen. "Here, relax for a few minutes while I clean up." He walked off down the hall.

Michelle watched Lafe leave the room, then she sat down on the sofa. Fighting a yawn, she placed her glass on the table and laid her head against the back cushions, closing her eyes. *Lord! It's been a long week.* At least she didn't have to go home and cook dinner. In fact, she could do whatever she wanted....

Ten minutes later Lafe had showered and changed into clean clothes. Still barefoot, he hurried back into the living room, afraid that Michelle might have gotten tired of waiting and taken off. Instead he found her on the sofa, sound asleep.

He smiled as he sat down beside her, remembering another night when she had conked out on him. He watched her peacefully sleeping and hated to have to wake her. He lowered his eyes to her full lips, which were parted slightly, just begging to be kissed. *Pull yourself together, Colter!* he reprimanded himself, and spoke her name softly.

Michelle made a murmuring sound and leaned toward him, searching for something to rest her head on. Lafe couldn't resist and closed the gap between them. He placed his arm across the back of the sofa as she snuggled against his chest. He froze, feeling his heart hammering wildly. *Well, you got what you wanted, guy—she's in your arms. Now what are you going to do?* Lafe just sat there, remembering another night a year ago, and a Colorado thunderstorm that had brought her into his arms...and into his thoughts more often than he wanted to admit.

He had built a fire to ward off the cool mountain air. On the rug in front of the hearth Michelle had clung to him as if she would never let go. He'd seen the fear in her brown eyes and suspected it went beyond the storm brewing outside his condominium. He'd stroked her, hoping to comfort, but before he knew it, his mouth was covering hers. The simple kiss had added fuel to the fire already rushing though his body. It had nearly killed him when she'd moaned and tried to move closer. If he'd let her it would have been all over. His body was aroused beyond human endurance.

Somehow he'd managed to break off the kiss, knowing it was for the best. Michelle had come to Glenwood Springs on business, for God's sake. She wasn't a one-night stand. Besides, her husband had been gone only a short time and Lafe didn't want the longing in her eyes to be for another man. So he'd forced himself to be content with holding her, until she'd fallen asleep. When the storm had ended, he'd carried her to her room and put her to bed...alone.

The following day, he'd tried to keep his distance, but Michelle was hard to resist. Since it was Sunday, they'd ended up spending the day sight-seeing. He'd shown her around the Glenwood Springs area, then they'd hiked to a special spot in the mountains and shared lunch. He'd never talked to anyone the way he had to Michelle that day. She, too, talked, some about her family, even about her husband's accident, but he'd sensed that the pain he saw in her eyes went deeper than her recent loss.

When she'd shown up in his bedroom that night he'd nearly gone crazy from wanting her. But he'd known it wasn't him she wanted. It might not have mattered with any other woman, but it had with Michelle. Turning her away was the hardest thing he ever had to do. It had been the only way to save himself.

Lafe shook away the memory as Michelle shifted position. Her arms stretched across his waist, hugging him close as her cheek rubbed against his chest.

Oh, God! Not again. This is going to kill me. Everywhere she touched him he was on fire. Lafe finally took a ragged breath, laid his head against the back of the sofa, aching to wrap his arms around her. He wanted to kiss her sweet mouth until she begged him for more, then he wanted to carry her into the bedroom and— *Stop it!* He ran a frustrated hand through his hair. *You've got to wake her.*

Lafe gently laid his arm on hers and for a second just enjoyed the feeling. Then he gave her a soft nudge. "Michelle..."

Michelle's eyes fluttered open and she looked at Lafe. She didn't move as their gazes held for a spellbinding moment. Then she pulled away. "I'm sorry," she apologized as she sat up straight, smoothing the wrinkles from her skirt. "I didn't mean to fall asleep."

Lafe took her hand. "Hey, don't worry about it. You've been working a lot of hours." He rubbed her small hand between his. "It's always that way in the beginning of a project. In a few weeks things will settle down."

"I guess so," she agreed as a rosy glow colored her cheeks, "but it's no excuse for falling asleep on your sofa."

"Let's not worry about it, okay?" He smiled. "I bet you need something to eat."

"Oh, no. There's no need—"

Lafe took her by the hand and escorted her into the kitchen. "This would be a good time to talk business. We seem to have been missing each other all week."

He turned to look at her; there was a glint of humor in his green eyes, she could see. "And I'd like you to come out to the site on Monday."

Michelle knew Lafe was right—she couldn't keep avoiding him. The setup work for Ocean Bluff was nearly completed. From now on she needed to be out at the site to keep a closer eye on things, get to know the subcontractors. And phone tag wasn't going to work any longer with Lafe. "I'll drive out after I stop by the office, probably about nine."

Michelle set the table while Lafe worked at chopping the vegetables for an omelet. Casually, as if he were trying to keep a conversation going, he began asking seemingly innocent questions.

She found herself telling Lafe about her relationship with the Staffords. How she'd met Betty in school and how the friendship had lasted until she'd married Tom. She didn't want to go any further; as far as she was concerned, all questions about her husband were off-limits. She didn't want anyone's pity. She steered the discussion back to a safe topic.

"Ben and Mary Stafford were rich, and we Donovans were as blue collar as possible. But it never seemed to make a difference in our friendship."

"It was the first thing I noticed about Ben," Lafe said as he carried the food to the table. "How evenhandedly he treats people." He returned to the counter and poured them both some coffee. "Here, this should help for your drive home."

"Thank you. I really need it tonight." She smiled and found she was looking forward to getting one in return. Lafe didn't disappoint her.

Michelle found it hard to breathe and she quickly picked up her fork and took a bite. "Mmm! This is really good. Where did you learn to cook?"

He shrugged. "Being single was a great incentive."

Michelle swallowed her food. "Boy, are you different. Most men think it's some sort of sin to go into a kitchen. Tom probably would have starved if he had to cook."

"I doubt that," Lafe disagreed. "If you get tired enough of fast food and hungry enough, you'll learn your way around the kitchen. Maybe you just spoiled your husband too much." He eyed her.

"I...I think it started with his mother." She looked down at her plate. Why did she say that?

"Tom was a lucky man."

"Oh, I bet your mother spoiled you a little, too," she teased, and glanced up to find Lafe's eyes turning cold and distant.

"I wouldn't know. Rosie May didn't hang around long enough to spoil me. She dumped me with my uncle and took off."

Michelle swallowed hard. Lafe had told her that his uncle had raised him, but she had just assumed his mother had died. Now she knew the cause of the pain she saw in his eyes. "I'm sorry" was all that she said; anything else would be construed as pity.

"Don't worry about it," he told her, brushing off her remark. "It happened so long ago that I hardly ever think about it."

There was little or no talking during the rest of the meal as they both concentrated on their food, then over coffee discussed business.

"If you wouldn't mind faxing me the list of subcontractors you hired," Michelle began, "I want to see if we're able to begin construction as early as the end of next week."

"May I ask why you're rushing the original starting date?" Lafe picked up the coffeepot and refilled their mugs. "We're already ahead of schedule."

Michelle shrugged. "You should know from experience, Lafe, that there are too many snags along the way that can hold up a job. I just want to make sure that we stay on schedule."

"But working fourteen-hour days can catch up with you," he chided, cradling his mug in his hands. That's one of the reasons I'm retiring from the business."

Michelle still found it hard to believe.

"Well, I'm happy if that's what you want. But I don't have the luxury right now. But as soon as Ocean Bluff is completed, I'll be able to take some time off."

"Is that what you tell your son?"

Michelle stiffened, not happy with Lafe questioning the way she raised her son. "T.J. understands."

"Does he ever get to see you these days?"

"Look, it's a fact of life that I have to work to support myself and my son. I need that bonus Ben promised if we finish on time." She thought about the things the extra money would go for, such as the balloon mortgage payment coming due next year, or starting a college fund for T.J.

Lafe leaned back in the chair and grinned. "Maybe you can buy a normal-size car."

"My car is running fine."

"Then maybe a vacation for you and T.J."

She bristled. He was getting too personal. "Maybe we can, but I have bills, Lafe, lots of bills to pay first before we can think of anything so frivolous as a vacation."

His face dropped. "Michelle, if things are tight, maybe I can help—"

"No. No, thank you." She tried to remain composed, not wanting anyone to know about her financial troubles. "T.J. and I are fine."

Lafe got up and went to her, but when he reached out to her she brushed away his hand. "Look, Lafe, I know this is difficult, especially since we have...a past." She drew a shaky breath. "We have to be able to put our personal feelings aside and work together."

"What if I can't, Michelle?"

She could only stare at him.

"If we only had a past I could handle it. But what happened between us is still there," he confessed. "You feel it, and I feel it."

He closed the distance between them, and before Michelle knew what was happening she was in his embrace.

The kiss caressed, wandered over her lips, touching, then pulling back and touching again. Lafe's strong arm tightened around her, then he deepened the kiss. She moaned as his tongue gained access, burying itself deeply in her mouth. Her arms wrapped around his neck, bringing him closer. Their tongues dueled, then she ran hers over his teeth before entering and tasting his mouth.

This time Lafe groaned and broke off the kiss. He held her tightly to his chest. "Oh, Michelle." He was breathing hard. "Can't you feel it?" He trailed kisses from her ear down her neck, causing her to shiver.

Michelle struggled with desire and finally managed to come to her senses. She jerked away, leaving the kitchen and heading back to the living room. "No! This is a mistake."

"I'd call it a lot of things...." He followed her closely. "But not a mistake. It's hot ... arousing ... makes me want to pull you down on the floor and make love—"

"Stop! I won't go to bed with you, Lafe."

"You didn't seem to have any problem with that a year ago. You came into my bedroom and offered yourself to me. Or was I just a ... a substitute for ... for someone else?"

Michelle fought back the pain and her tears. "That was a long time ago. I've changed. I don't need a man to make my life complete."

"It's lonely out there, Michelle." Lafe looked angry. "I know, I've spent my whole life on my own, concentrating on my business until there was nothing else."

"But I *need* to make it on my own. I've worked hard to become project manager. Ocean Bluff may be your last job before you retire. It's my future." It's what makes me feel alive, she thought, still shaking from the kiss. She went to the sofa and picked up her purse. She studied the confident man standing in the doorway. Would he ever be able to understand why this job was so important to her? "I'll resign if we can't manage a working relationship."

Lafe was used to being in control, and he didn't like the tables being turned on him. But, as much as he hated it, he knew she was right. "You got it."

Michelle hurried past him toward the door. "I'll be at the site on Monday."

Lafe's gaze followed Michelle until the front door slammed shut. He listened for her car to start and pull out of the driveway. Things had changed. This time he hadn't sent her away. She'd walked out on her own. But he knew things between them weren't settled. Their kiss had proven that.

No, Michelle Royer definitely wasn't out of his system.

Chapter Four

Michelle pulled her car off the main highway onto the dirt road that led to the site. After carefully maneuvering the VW around several potholes for the next half mile, she spotted the sign Stafford Investments. Farther down the road the construction trailer came into view. Colter Construction was printed boldly on the side. Nearby there were several tidy stacks of lumber, two-by-fours ready for framing the structures.

This must be the place, she thought as she parked her car along the row of heavy equipment. Michelle felt the excitement building as she got out of her car. This was her project. Ocean Bluff. She couldn't keep a grin off her face as she glanced around and saw the earth movers busy at work, but the grin quickly disappeared when her gaze wandered toward the trailer and the familiar blue Bronco parked next to it. Well, he was here, waiting for her, just as he'd promised.

Michelle drew a long breath, but it didn't help relieve her tension. All she could think about was Friday night and Lafe's kiss. It had been the same the entire weekend. The man had caused her to lose sleep. Every time she closed her eyes she saw his face and that cocky grin of his.

"Please Lafe! Please keep your distance," she muttered as she grabbed her purse and briefcase off the seat. After shutting the car door, she walked off toward the construction trailer, berating herself for not changing her clothes after the lenders meeting that morning. At least she could have brought along some practical shoes, she thought as she felt her heels sink into the sandy terrain.

Michelle shaded her eyes from the bright sunlight and began looking around the site. The last time she had been there Chris had driven out, but they hadn't had time that day to even get out of the car. She was to the rear of the land parcels, a little too far back to get the full view, but that didn't stop her as she started off toward the bluff. She ignored the fact that she was dressed in her best navy suit, and that her skirt was pencil slim, and that some of the crew gave her strange looks as she trudged past in high heels. She didn't care. She wanted to see if the buyers were really getting the promised million-dollar view.

When Michelle reached the edge of the rocky bluff, she stopped in her tracks, spellbound. The constant wind brushed her hair from her face and waffled her skirt against her legs as she studied the breathtaking view. Below the thirty-foot cliff was the Pacific Ocean, its aquamarine waves rolling restlessly toward the deserted beach. She glanced up and down the area, not finding a soul in sight. "It's absolutely beautiful," Michelle whispered almost reverently.

"I have to agree with you."

Startled, Michelle whirled around, to find Lafe standing behind her. He had on faded jeans and a blue chambray shirt. He wore his tan work boots, and sitting on his head was a bright yellow hard hat. A second hat was in his hands. He looked angry.

"Lafe, I was just coming to see you." She felt her cheeks warm as she glanced away from his intense stare. "I guess I got distracted."

"Next time stop by the trailer and pick up one of these." He held out the other hard hat. "You know the rules, Michelle." He stepped closer, placed the hat on her head and pushed it down until it fitted snugly.

She tried to hide her embarrassment, but knew her fair skin betrayed her. "You're right. I guess I wasn't thinking."

There was an awkward moment as they both stood there, then Lafe looked out over the cliff. "It's easy to get distracted by this view."

"Think what it would be like to live out here." Michelle sighed. It would have been heaven to play here when she was a child.

"Well, no one's going to be living here if we don't get busy," Lafe said, breaking through her daydream. "Did you bring that list of suppliers?" He turned and started toward the trailer.

Michelle had no choice but to follow.

"Yes, I did." She tried to keep up with his long strides, but in her shoes it was nearly impossible. She made a note to herself to keep a pair of shoes in her car—along with a hard hat. All at once her foot sank in a small hole and she gasped. Just as she started to fall, Lafe grabbed her and pulled her against him. Once she'd regained her balance, he reached down and grasped her ankle, studying her three-inch heel. "I don't think these were designed for this kind of terrain."

Michelle found it difficult to speak with Lafe's warm hand cradling her calf. "Sorry, I had an important meeting this morning," she explained. "I guess I should have brought a change of clothes."

To Michelle's relief, Lafe released her leg and stood, tipping his hard hat off his forehead.

"I suggest you invest in some sturdy boots before you break a leg."

Then, before Michelle knew what he was planning, he swung her up into his arms. Catching the familiar scent of his after-shave, she nearly forgot to resist. She recovered quickly, trying to balance her purse and briefcase. "Lafe, put me down. This isn't necessary, really. I can walk."

"For once, Michelle, stop arguing, before we both end up in the dirt."

"I'd rather end up in the dirt than have the construction crew see the contractor carrying the project manager. How many other project managers have you had to carry because their high heels got stuck in the mud?"

Lafe watched as Michelle clamped her lips together and glared at him. But he wasn't thinking about why he should put her down, just how it felt as her shapely hips pressed against his midsection and her breast came in direct contact with his chest. Damn! Common sense told him he shouldn't have touched her, shouldn't have gotten within fifty yards of the woman, knowing the effect she had on him. But she felt so damn good in his arms.

Once they reached the rise on the cliff Lafe stopped, then set Michelle on her feet. He watched as she straightened her clothes and looked up at him.

"Thank you," she said too politely. She turned and carefully struggled through the soft soil toward the trailer. When she started to fall once again, Lafe rushed to her side.

"Lady, you need rescuing whether you like it or not." He tried to take her arm, only to have Michelle push it away. Instead she handed him her briefcase to hold. Then she leaned down and pulled off her high heels. Tossing Lafe a knowing look, she continued the journey in her stocking feet.

The next week, Michelle drove her car through her tree-lined neighborhood. She had grown up in the area, and loved her small clapboard-and-stucco house in the older part of Santa Ana. Although some of the houses were faded and needed minor repairs, the middle-class homes had been kept up over the years.

She sighed. It had been another long day, and she was looking forward to a peaceful evening. For the next few hours she was going to forget about work and concentrate on spending some time with her son. No more Ocean Bluff, no Lafe....

She glanced at her watch, to see that it was after six o'clock. Was he still working at the site? she wondered. She hadn't seen him since he'd tried to carry her to the trailer.

Michelle's heart began to pound as she remembered the feel of his strong arms and solid chest. Quickly shaking off her thoughts, she turned onto her street. Time to put business and Lafe Colter out of her head.

She pulled into the driveway and smiled, seeing her brother's truck. It had been a while since Joe had come by to visit. He was probably after a free meal.

Inside the house Michelle found T.J. and Joe playing a video game. "Hello, I'm home," she called over the sounds of guns firing on the TV screen.

"Mom," T.J. said, getting up to give his mother a kiss.

This was worth all the hard work. She hugged her son tightly, knowing that in a few years he wouldn't be so eager to greet her this way. She stood back and looked at him. T.J. was the image of his father. He had the same blue eyes and wayward blond curls. She brushed the hair off his forehead. When he smiled his mouth revealed two missing bottom teeth and one on the top.

"Mom, look!" The boy pointed toward the television. "Uncle Joe bought a new video game. It's really neat." He went back to his game.

"I bet it is," Michelle murmured as her brother walked toward her. How many times had she asked her family to stop spoiling T.J. with presents? She raised up and gave Joe a kiss on the cheek. "What brings you to this side of town? Did Dad send you to check up on me?"

"No, just thought I'd stop by and see how you and the kid are doing." Joe shrugged. "I've missed a lot of years of seeing my nephew growing up."

Although Michelle tried not to dwell on it, she never wanted to forget her life with Tom, or that she wasn't the only person who had suffered under his control. "You know you're welcome here whenever you want to come by. And you don't even have to buy T.J. a present."

"I didn't—the game is mine."

Joseph Donovan stood six-foot-one. His body was lean, and even at the age of thirty-two, without an ounce of excess fat. His head tilted down toward her, revealing he was in need of a haircut. Curly auburn hair fell well over his ears and below his nape.

"When did you buy a Nintendo?"

"That's the best part. I didn't have to. I'll just come over here and borrow T.J.'s."

"Yeah, isn't it great," she said, trying not to smile. "And while you're here maybe I can fix you some dinner."

Joe gave her the heart-stopping Donovan grin. "I was hoping you'd take pity on a poor bachelor."

"Poor?" Michelle gave him a doubtful look, folding her arms across her chest. "Oh, Joey, what am I going to do with you?"

"Feed me some of that wonderful casserole Margaret put in the oven before she left to go play bingo."

"Oh, no, Margaret!" Michelle felt bad. Her widowed neighbor loved watching T.J. after school, but maybe the long hours were getting to be too much. "I should have gotten home earlier."

"Michelle, Margaret understands you have to work. Besides, I told her that whenever she has to leave early just to call me and I'll come and watch T.J." Joe placed his arm across her shoulder and guided her into the small kitchen. "C'mon, sis, I'll help you make a salad, and you can tell me how you weaseled the job of boss for this Ocean Bluff project."

"Try it now," Joe called from behind the VW.

Michelle sat in the driver's seat and turned the key as instructed. When the engine came to life, she looked back at her brother as he squatted before the engine. Stepping out of the car, she joined him, handing Joe the tools he needed to adjust the carburetor. This had been a common occurrence with Michelle and Joe. She was forever hanging around the garage with her brothers, where she'd picked up quite a bit about cars.

Michelle listened to the smooth purr of the Bug's engine. "Sounds great."

"Did you have any doubts?" Joe raised an eyebrow.

"No. You seem to be able to perform miracles." She remembered the miracle he'd performed after rescuing this car from the junkyard. "Thanks again." She hugged him.

Joe returned the hug, then whispered in her ear, "Hey, sis. Do you know a man about six feet tall, wears a cowboy hat, has lots of muscles—and a very angry expression on his face?"

"What are you talking about?" Michelle pulled back from their embrace and gazed in the direction Joe was pointing.

Michelle looked toward the back of the garage, to find Lafe Colter standing in the doorway. His broad shoulders were accented by the dark fitted western shirt he wore, just as his snug jeans emphasized his slim waist. In his hands he held a straw cowboy hat.

"Lafe." Her voice was gravelly. She swallowed. "What are you doing here? Is there something wrong at the site?"

"No, Michelle," Lafe answered quickly as he moved into the garage. "Everything is fine. I tried to catch you at the office, but you'd already left."

Michelle's heart began pumping faster as he came closer. What was he doing at her house? "How...did you find out where I live?"

"Your secretary gave me directions," he explained, but his gaze was riveted on Joe. "I need the list for the subcontractors again, and Peggy said you'd probably brought it home."

"I gave you the list last week."

"I guess I misplaced it," he admitted, embarrassed. "Would you have an extra copy? I have an electrical contractor who had to pull out."

Michelle had trouble concentrating on what he was saying. "Sure, it's in the house."

Lafe turned back to Joe again. "I apologize for intruding on your evening."

Michelle had forgotten about Joe. "I'm sorry. Lafe Colter, I'd like you to meet Joe Donovan—my brother."

Lafe blinked, an incredulous look on his face. "Your brother? You're brother and sister?"

"Have been for nearly thirty years." Joe extended a hand toward Lafe. "Nice to meet you. How's your truck these days? Sorry I wasn't there when you picked it up at the shop."

"It's running just fine, thank you." Lafe shook Joe's hand as he glanced back and forth between the two. "I should have seen the family resemblance. I guess the red hair and blue eyes had me confused."

"Michelle's the black sheep of the family," Joe teased.

"You'd better watch it," she warned, "or you'll never eat a meal around here again."

Michelle left Joe in the garage as she motioned Lafe to follow her into the house. Crossing through the kitchen, she was embarrassed at the stack of dirty dishes in the sink, but she hid the feeling by asking Lafe if he wanted coffee. After his refusal they continued into the dining room, where her briefcase sat on top a small secretary in the corner. Opening it, she quickly sorted through the papers, all the while feeling uneasy with Lafe in her home. She had resigned herself to working with the man, but that was at the office. His being here made her feel vulnerable again.

She glanced over her shoulder, to find him staring out the window into the darkness. Something squeezed Michelle's heart as she saw the faraway expression on his face. He looked so... alone. Though they had spent three days together in Colorado, she actually knew very little about the man, except that he had grown up on a ranch. She didn't know much about the man under the cowboy exterior.

Lafe must have felt her scrutiny, because he turned and his intense gaze locked with hers.

"I... I can't seem to find them," Michelle stammered. "I'll check my bedroom." She hurried off down the hall.

Lafe breathed a sigh. Coming here tonight had been a bad idea. He shouldn't have let Peggy talk him into driving to Michelle's house unannounced. Ever since his arrival, she had let him know that he was not wanted in her private life.

Hell, he should have just waited until tomorrow and contacted Michelle at the office. He began to pace. He should have just gone home; his concentration had been nonexistent the past few days. It was all the fault of one doe-eyed vixen named Michelle Royer.

It had been over a week since he'd seen her at the site. With their busy schedules, they had to communicate through faxes and phone messages. But she'd never been far from his thoughts. In fact, she managed to ruin his entire weekend. Maybe he should have flown to the ranch and worked off some of his frustrations by digging fence posts. He knew he had a capable foreman to handle those things, but Lafe always liked to do physical work when he had something on his mind. And he definitely had something on his mind.

He hadn't let a woman get to him like this in a long time. Not since high school, and Judy Simmons had taught him a hard lesson. Back then it had been overactive hormones, but it still hurt when she'd chosen someone else over him, just as his mother had. When he'd left the ranch for a rodeo career, most women he met only wanted the excitement of the winning ride, but didn't want to hang around for the long haul. Later, he'd played it safe and never allowed himself to get too close to anyone. In most of the relationships he'd had over the years, he had always had control. When he'd felt the need to move on, he had.

He looked around the cozy home that Michelle had shared with her husband and son. An overpowering sense of longing took over as he touched the lace cloth on the dining room table. There had been a lot of things that he'd lacked growing up. And with the passing of his thirty-sixth birthday, Lafe realized that there was more than work. Now, with his ranch and more than enough money to get by comfortably, he was going to take the time to enjoy life. He just chose to do it on his own.

"Hey, Mom! Can I go get some ice cream with Uncle Joe?"

Lafe swung around as Michelle's son came rushing into the room. Dressed in jeans and a T-shirt, the seven-year old was tossing a baseball up in the air, awkwardly trying to catch it in a mitt that looked three sizes too big. On his head was perched a California Angels cap. The boy came to an abrupt halt, his expression wary.

Lafe's mouth twitched. "Hi, I'm Lafe Colter. I work with your mother."

That didn't seem to impress him. "Is my mom your boss?"

Lafe came down on one knee so they could be eye level. "Let's just say she tells me what needs to be built, and I build it." He held out his hand. "You must be T.J. Royer."

The boy hesitated, but finally nodded, all the time examining Lafe closely. Then at last he shook his hand. "You a real cowboy?" Lafe glanced down at his state of dress — jeans, boots and the straw Stetson he was holding in his hands. "I guess I am."

"Do you have a horse, too?"

"I have a few on my ranch."

That did it. T.J.'s eyes sparkled. "Do you have cattle on your ranch. Ever been in a rodeo and ride a bucking bronc?"

"Whoa, partner." Lafe held up his hand. "One thing at a time. I have some cattle. And yes, I've ridden on a bucking bronc, but that was sometime ago."

"Wow! Is your ranch close? Can I see it?"

Before Lafe could answer the next round of questions, he looked up and saw Michelle standing in the doorway. She came up to her son and drew him against her side. "T.J., stop asking Mr. Colter so many questions. He's in a hurry."

Smiling, Lafe stood up. "I can spare the time to answer him." He looked back to the boy. "My ranch is in Colorado."

T.J. appeared forlorn. "That's far away, isn't it? My mom flew there once on an airplane."

Lafe tugged on the boy's cap. "Maybe someday you can come for a visit, too."

"You mean it? Really?"

"Sure do," Lafe said, then looked at Michelle. She was not happy with his invitation.

"Wow!"

"T.J.," Michelle interrupted. "Why don't you go to the garage and see what your uncle is doing, while I talk with Mr. Colter."

"Oh, yeah, he wants to take me for ice cream. Can I go?"

Michelle sighed. "Sure, honey, but remember there's school tomorrow."

T.J. smiled. "Thanks, Mom. Bye, Mr. Colter." The boy waved as he hurried out the door.

Lafe didn't know what had come over him. "Hey, T.J., if you're interested, I have tickets for the Angels game next week. Maybe you and your mom would want to go."

"Wow! Would I! Thanks, Mr. Colter." The boy hurried out the back door.

"Here." Michelle glared at Lafe as she shoved him the list. "Sorry it took so long."

Lafe felt Michelle's reprimand even without any words. "Look, I apologize. I shouldn't have invited T.J. to the ranch without asking you first. But when I saw his enthusiasm..."

"I thought we agreed to keep our relationship business-like. And you come here and ask my son to go visit you in Colorado." He watched as Michelle closed her eyes and drew a long breath. "Now I'm going to have to be the bad guy and tell T.J. he can't go."

"But why? There's no reason you couldn't come this summer." For some reason Lafe felt it was important they visit the ranch.

Michelle just glared at him again, but said nothing.

"Well, I'd better go," he said, and walked toward the door. "Tell T.J. the Angels game is Friday night. I'll pick you both up about six."

"Lafe, didn't I make myself clear?" She hurried after him. "We work together."

"There's no reason we can't go as friends," he countered with a smile. "Besides, it's one way I can guarantee that you won't be working after-hours. Plus you'll be spending the evening with your son." He placed his hat on his head and walked out the door.

Michelle sat down on the sofa, lost in thought. Lafe had her confused and totally off balance. Just thinking about the way he'd looked tonight, the way he'd smiled at her, had her heart pounding as if she had jogged for miles.

She closed her eyes, and the memories came flooding back. Memories of a time when her total focus had had to be on Tom. Even her child's needs had never been able to come before her husband's. The years that his verbal, and occasionally physical, abuse had had her cowering at her own shadow. When she had been notified of Tom's death, Michelle wasn't as much saddened as she was relieved. It was finally over. The love she had once felt for Tom Royer had faded long before he'd crashed his car on the mountain road.

But her pain wasn't over. She lived day after day, blaming herself for what had happened to her marriage. Her wounds were starting to heal, but there would always be emotional scars.

A tear fell down her cheek, and she brushed it away quickly. Loving wasn't supposed to hurt like that. She bit down on her lower lip. Her thoughts turned once more to Lafe Colter. Never would she let herself be hurt again, she vowed. Never... Never....

Early the next morning, Michelle marched up the steps and knocked on the trailer door.

"Come in" she heard a voice call out.

Jerking open the door, she found Lafe sitting behind his desk, going over some blueprints. Well, too bad, she decided. She needed to get her point across, and he was going to listen to her.

"Lafe, we need to talk," she began when he jerked his head up in surprise. Good, she had caught him off guard. "I didn't like what you did, not one bit. You had no right, Lafe."

He frowned at her. "Had no right to what?"

"You had no right telling *my son* that you were going to take him to Colorado."

Michelle drew a needed breath, but when Lafe tried to speak she raised her hand to silence him. He nodded and leaned back in his chair, crossing his arms over his chest. "First of all, the idea is ridiculous. Second, don't you dare ask T.J. to go somewhere without asking me first."

"Got it," Lafe agreed.

His quick answer caught Michelle off guard. "Good. Now that we got that straightened out—" she walked to the desk and laid her briefcase on top "—I brought the budget cost sheets and..." Her words died out as she looked up to find someone sitting on the couch. A young man with light brown hair, brown eyes and a contagious grin that showed straight white teeth. Jeff Brown, Lafe's foreman.

"Jeff? I didn't know..." She felt herself blushing. "Lafe didn't tell me you were going to be working here."

"I don't think he got the chance," Jeff teased, and she blushed harder. "How are you, Michelle?" The young man stood and took her hand and shook it. "Good to see you again."

"Nice to see you, too," she answered honestly, remembering how kind he'd been to her in Glenwood Springs.

He glanced at Lafe. "I see you two are still going at it. Maybe it's a good thing I'm here to referee."

Lafe stood, came around the desk and sat down on the edge. "We were doing fine until you showed up."

Grinning, Jeff shook his head. "Yeah, I could see that. The sparks are still flying."

Michelle's and Lafe's eyes locked for a second, then she glanced away.

Lafe cleared his throat. "Jeff, why don't you go check on the delivery. I heard the truck pull in a few minutes ago." He handed Jeff a copy of the supply order. The foreman headed out the door, leaving Lafe and Michelle alone.

Lafe turned his attention to Michelle while she searched through her briefcase. He bit back a grin recalling her entrance. Her Irish temper was working overtime, and it always seemed to be directed at him. His body heated as he watched her slim skirt hug her nicely shaped hips. He moved his gaze to her low shoes that did nothing to deter from the graceful curve of her legs. She swung around as if she realized he'd been watching her. Her dark silky hair brushed her shoulders while her eyes raised to meet his. She was one helluva lovely lady.

"I... I'd better be getting back. I put the budget sheet on your desk," she said, picking up her things. As she turned and started for the door, Lafe panicked. He couldn't let her leave.

"Michelle."

When she glanced over her shoulder Lafe almost lost his nerve. Almost. "I still have the Angels tickets for Friday night."

Her delicate mouth dropped open and it gave Lafe the most erotic thoughts.

"I thought we'd decided it would be best—"

"No," he interrupted. "You decided. I decided I would love to take you and T.J. to the ball game."

"But, Lafe, we work together. I told you that I don't want to mix business with pleasure."

Lafe decided to use a little charm, and he smiled. "So you think that going out with me would be a pleasure?"

"Don't put words into my mouth. It's not a good idea."

"C'mon, Michelle. I'm not asking you to go away for the weekend." He watched her tense. "I'm asking you and your son to a baseball game with twenty thousand other people around. I don't know what I can possibly do in that crowd. Unless you're embarrassed to be seen with me. If I promise to ditch the hat and boots, would you be willing to be seen with me?" This time he tossed her his best grin. It worked, and she started to smile.

"Okay, T.J. and I will go to the game with you." She opened the door, but stopped when he called to her.

He raised his hand in the air. "I'll be on my best behavior."

Michelle lifted an eyebrow. "Lafe, I suggest you don't make promises you can't keep."

Chapter Five

"Hey, fella, you need glasses. He was out by a mile," Michelle shouted, cupping her hands around her mouth so she could be heard over the other twenty-five-thousand-plus fans in Anaheim Stadium booing the second-base umpire's call. Still on her feet, she glanced over her shoulder, to find Lafe sitting calmly alongside T.J. Well, maybe not everyone was booing.

"Sorry, I guess I get a little carried away."

"You're not bothering me," Lafe stated as he popped a shelled peanut into his mouth, then turned to the boy. "Your mother bothering you?"

"No." T.J. copied Lafe by dropping a peanut into his mouth, too. "She's fun to go to a game with. She lets me yell all I want. And when my permanent teeth come in, Mom's going to teach me how to whistle really loud," the boy said as he held up his pinkies. "You have to use these two fingers."

"You do?" Lafe presented two different fingers. "I use these two." Then he placed them in his mouth and blew a sharp whistle. "That's to call my horse."

"Wow!" T.J. examined Lafe's fingers as if they held magical powers. "You think you could teach me?"

"Sure, anytime you want." Lafe realized he really wanted to teach the boy. He raised his gaze to discover that Michelle was watching him. What surprised him was the smile she had on her face.

"What's wrong?"

"Nothing." She shook her head. "I'm just having a good time. Thank you for bringing us to the game."

"It's my pleasure." When his gaze held hers, Lafe found he had trouble remaining passive. His body was already betraying him. He quickly shifted position on the hard seat and turned his attention to the child jumping up and cheering for the Angels base hit. "You have a great son, Michelle. Your husband would have been proud of him."

Her smile faded. "To be honest, nothing much pleased Tom." Then, as if she'd said too much, Michelle turned her attention to the game.

Lafe sat there, wondering if her and Tom's marriage was as perfect as he'd always thought or had been led to believe. He eyed the seven-year-old seated next to him. What man wouldn't be proud of a son like T.J.? If the boy were his...

Whoa. Lafe suddenly stopped himself. He'd never thought about having a child before. He had always been too busy with his construction business, and now he had his ranch. Of course, once he was retired he would have all the time in the world to show someone how to ride a horse, maybe even to rope. Back when he'd been doing the rodeo circuit, he'd done pretty good in calf roping.

All at once he felt a tugging on his arm and looked down at T.J. seated next to him. The boy crooked his finger and Lafe leaned closer to hear what the child had to say.

"Mr. Colter, will you take me to the bathroom? Please. My mom won't let me go by myself and...and..."

Lafe saw the child's uneasiness as he glanced at his mother.

"Sure, we can go together. I was thinking about heading up there myself." Lafe stood and T.J. took hold of his hand.

A sudden rush of emotion caught in Lafe's throat as the trusting child allowed him to lead him up the steps.

"Hey, where you two going?" Michelle called after them.

Lafe glanced down at T.J. and winked. "We're going to stop by the refreshment stand and get some ice cream. Is that okay?"

"Sure, why not," Michelle agreed. It would nicely top off the hot dog, two bags of peanuts and popcorn her son had devoured earlier.

She leaned back in her seat and tried to watch the game, but her mind was on the two guys heading for the concession stand. Most of the evening they'd been in deep conversation. She figured her son was probably asking Lafe questions about his ranch. She smiled. Even as a toddler, T.J. had been crazy about cowboys, wearing an old cowboy hat whose brim drooped and kept falling in his face.

Now her child seemed enthralled with every word Lafe had to say. This was one of those times when Michelle felt guilty that she couldn't give her son what he so desperately needed. Male attention. Besides her father and brothers, there probably wasn't going to be another man in her or her son's life.

Her thoughts immediately went to Lafe Colter and their encounter in Colorado. How easily she had succumbed to him, she realized as she thought back to the way Lafe had held her so tenderly that first night. How he had listened while she'd cried through her pain. If only Tom had been more like—

Hearing the familiar voices, she turned toward the aisle as Lafe and T.J. came back to their seats, both licking large ice-cream cones. She rolled her eyes, knowing her son would probably have one huge stomachache that night. But she didn't care; he was having a lot of fun. This time Lafe took the seat next to hers, juggling two vanilla cones. The ice cream was already melting and running down the sides.

"Here, this one's for you." Lafe started to hand it to her, then pulled it back and took a quick lick off the side to prevent more from dropping. "Hope you like vanilla."

Michelle stared at the cone, knowing it was silly to react to Lafe's action. It seemed so...so familiar, as if they were closer than just...business associates. She came back to reality when the cone threatened to drip again.

"I love any flavor," she answered, before running her tongue around the edge. When she looked back at Lafe, he was staring at her intently. There was a tingling in the pit of her stomach as his gaze moved over her like a soft caress. She had to fight the overwhelming need to reach out and touch—

Suddenly there was a cracking sound and the crowd stood up around them, cheering. But they remained in their seats. It wasn't until T.J. spoke that they broke eye contact.

"Did you see it?" the boy said excitedly. "The Angels hit a home run."

Embarrassed, Michelle glanced away. It was Lafe who answered T.J. "Sure did, son. Looks like we're going to win."

The boy grinned, still holding on to his ice cream. "Isn't it great, Mr. Colter? Thanks for bringing me."

"You're welcome, T.J. But don't you think we're good-enough friends now that you can call me Lafe?"

"Wow!" T.J. turned to his mother. "Can I, Mom?"

Michelle jerked her head around as panic raced through her. She definitely didn't want Lafe getting this friendly.

Lafe picked the sleeping child up out of the back seat of the Bronco and followed Michelle into the house.

"His room is down the hall," Michelle explained as she led the way. Inside the room, she turned on the small light next to the bed and pulled the comforter back. She walked to the dresser as Lafe laid the child down. Returning with a pair of pajamas, she began pulling off the child's shoes. T.J. began to mumble and turned to his side.

"T.J., c'mon, honey. Let me get you undressed."

"No! I can do it," he grumbled sleepily. "Not a baby anymore."

Lafe smiled, seeing Michelle's frustration. Looked like her son had inherited her stubbornness.

"I know you're not a baby, but you're too tired to get undressed."

"Don't want to wear pajamas. They're dumb. Bet Lafe doesn't wear pajamas." T.J. managed to open his eyes and focus on Lafe.

"Well, Mr. Colter." Michelle folded her arms across her chest and glared at him. "Please don't keep us in suspense."

Lafe held back a groan as he tried to figure a way out of this one. He doubted that Michelle would like it if he confessed he didn't wear anything to bed. Of course he'd love to see the look on her face. "Why don't you let me help T.J. get ready for bed?"

He watched as Michelle struggled with the idea, then finally she relented, leaving them alone.

Lafe sat down on the edge of the bed. "First of all, T.J., a cowboy never argues with his mother, especially after she was nice enough to let you go to the game."

The child looked ashamed. "I'm sorry."

"You tell her. First thing in the morning," Lafe suggested. "Second. There is nothing wrong with pajamas."

The child raised his head. "Do you sleep in them?"

"Well, not usually, but I live alone. I think your mother would appreciate you wearing something, instead of running around in your birthday suit."

The boy giggled. "That's funny."

"Oh, it is?" Lafe began tickling the child and they ended up wrestling around on the bed. "Well, I think this is funny. Say 'uncle.'"

"Uncle, uncle!"

Lafe stopped and watched the smiling boy as he began to yawn. "Why don't you just sleep in your underwear?" That seemed to satisfy the boy, and he sat up and let Lafe remove his shirt and jeans. T.J. crawled under the blanket and yawned once again.

"You all set now?"

T.J. lay on his back and pulled his arms from under the blanket, playing with the satin ribbing along the edge.

"Lafe, do you think that I could…maybe hug you just one time?"

Lafe was too startled by the boy's suggestion to offer any objection. "Sure." He swallowed as T.J. sat up and reached around his neck, gripping him tightly. Lafe found he was holding on, too. Is this what he'd been missing all these years? he wondered as the child let go.

"My daddy didn't like to hug" was all T.J. said as he climbed back under the blankets. "'Night."

Lafe sat there for a moment in the dimly-lit room, trying to understand what T.J. was saying. Of course he could relate to the boy about hugs. He couldn't ever remember getting any. His mother hardly showed him any affection, and his Uncle Ray never. Lafe had always told himself he didn't need it. He glanced down at the sleeping child and a knot tightened in his chest. He'd been wrong.

Assured that T.J. was asleep, Lafe left the room and walked toward the other end of the house in search of Michelle. He found her in the kitchen, making coffee.

She turned around as Lafe leaned his tall frame against the counter in the small room. "Would you like a cup?"

"Sure, I have a long drive home."

Michelle studied the man for a moment, wondering how he could look so good in worn jeans and a navy polo shirt. She glanced down at his feet and found the rattiest pair of tennis shoes. He'd kept his promise, though, not to wear his boots and hat. "Well, what did T.J. decide to sleep in?" She handed him a steaming mug.

"His underwear."

Michelle grimaced. "He'll probably kick off his blankets in the middle of the night and freeze."

"And by tomorrow he'll realize pj's are fine," Lafe said, and took a sip from his cup.

"In case you haven't noticed it, Lafe, my son has a big case of hero worship. He'll want to wear what you wear."

Lafe cupped his mug in his hand. "Well, then he'll really get cold, because I don't sleep in anything." He cocked an eyebrow. "If you'd walked into my room a few minutes later that night in Glenwood Springs you would have discovered that for yourself."

Michelle nearly choked on her coffee. She tried to stay calm and composed. But how could she, when the image of Lafe Colter wrapped in a towel—or nothing!—kept playing in her mind?

"Lafe, I'd appreciate it if you wouldn't keep bringing that up. It's in the...past." The words were hard to get out of her dry throat.

"How about if we talk about something else, then? Like Tom Royer?"

Michelle became more uncomfortable as her dismay grew. "I really don't want to talk about my husband."

"You mean *perfect* husband, don't you."

"I never said Tom was perfect," she denied, wanting to run out of the room.

"You led me to believe it." He came closer. "How many others did you not allow to see Tom's true side?"

Michelle moved back. Dear God! Why was he doing this? "Our marriage wasn't anybody else's business."

Lafe was in front of her, his hand resting against the counter on either side of her as if holding her prisoner. She couldn't stand it and pushed his hand away. Lafe didn't resist and she moved across to the other side of the kitchen.

"Was he abusive to you and T.J.?"

"No!" she answered, almost too quickly. "Why would you ask that?"

Lafe studied her for a moment. "Just things you've said, and tonight T.J...."

"T.J. what?"

"T.J. asked me if I would mind if he gave me a hug." Lafe's eyes met hers. "He said his father didn't like hugs."

Michelle covered her trembling lips with her hand, hoping she could keep back her tears. It didn't work. "Oh, God!" She spun away, but Lafe was at her side. Although she resisted, he pulled her into his arms. She began to sob and nothing she did could stop the tears. Lafe just held her, letting her cry out her pain. Michelle finally raised her head to see an encouraging smile on his face.

"Tom and I married young," she began, stepping back and taking a tissue from the box on the counter to wipe her eyes. She looked at Lafe.

"When I got pregnant, Tom wasn't happy. Said he never wanted children and asked me to get an abortion."

Lafe clenched his fists. "That bastard."

Michelle flushed at his harsh words. "Of course I wouldn't even consider it. I also thought that once the baby was born things might change. I hoped that Tom would take one look at his child and..." Her voice drifted off.

"Michelle, you can't blame yourself for the way Tom felt," Lafe stressed. He knew from his own experience that some people were just too selfish.

"I thought I made up for his father's lack of attention." She sighed and wiped her eyes again. "I guess I didn't do as good a job as I thought."

"You're wrong, Michelle. You've done a great job with T.J." So many things made sense to Lafe now. Her turning to him in Colorado, and her not wanting anything to do with him since then. Lafe found he wanted to change her mind.

He brushed back a strand of hair. "You can't keep blaming yourself."

Michelle raised her eyes to meet his. It was a mistake. She swallowed anxiously as his hands cupped her face and his mouth came down to meet hers.

"Oh, Lafe," she groaned as her eyes fluttered and finally shut. His lips were soft, tender, as they caressed her mouth. Her legs suddenly felt all rubbery, and she had to grip his arms for support.

Lafe lifted his head and feathered kisses on her closed eyelids, then began nibbling on her neck. "God! You smell so good...and you taste so good." He pressed his hips to hers, making her aware of how much he wanted her.

Michelle was jolted back to reality. "Lafe. Please," she begged as she pushed him away. "No. We have to stop."

Lafe combed his fingers through his hair in frustration. "Listen to me, Michelle. We nearly found something good a year ago."

"No, Lafe. I can't. I just can't."

"Why not? You just proved that you have feelings for me."

She shook her head. "I don't want a man in my life. I have my career. That and T.J. are all that matters."

"No, we matter, too," he insisted. "Aren't you just a little curious about where it will lead?"

"All I'm curious about is how to keep our relationship strictly business and finish Ocean Bluff."

Monday morning Michelle felt miserable as she drove to work. She had planned to catch up on much-needed sleep over the weekend, but it hadn't worked out that way. Every time she had closed her eyes, her thoughts had turned to Lafe—how he'd held her in his arms, the taste of his mouth on hers. Dear Lord! She was doing it again.

That wasn't all she was concerned about. Since getting up Saturday morning, T.J. had been talking nonstop about Lafe. Worst of all her son wanted to invite him to one of his Little League games. Michelle had been able to talk T.J. into waiting awhile, explaining that Lafe was too busy with Ocean Bluff. But she knew from experience that the child would not be put off forever.

How was she going to keep her distance from the man, when he continued to involve himself in her personal life? He had even called her over the weekend to ask how she was doing.

"Well, Mr. Colter, this has got to stop," she recited under her breath, parking her VW next to Lafe's truck at the construction site. She checked her appearance in the rearview mirror, then climbed out of the car and walked toward the trailer. She had to get used to the idea that she was working with Lafe, and stop acting like a silly schoolgirl every time he smiled at her. She definitely had to quit staring at his body as though she'd never seen muscles before. For goodness' sake, she'd grown up with two brothers...and she had been married.

She paused on the step and sighed tiredly. It was going to be a long day, she thought, looking around the site at the Monday-morning activity. To her surprise she saw there were cement trucks parked, all set to lay the foundations. So soon? Suddenly her spirits lifted. They were ahead of schedule. She watched as the foreman, Jeff Brown, gave orders to begin pouring the concrete. Smiling, she knocked on the trailer door, then pushed it open. She walked inside to find Lafe sitting on the edge of the desk, talking on the phone.

Lafe's heart rate escalated when Michelle came through the door. She was dressed in a pair of navy pleated slacks and a cream-colored blouse. On her small feet, she wore low-heeled shoes. She had on very little makeup, and her hair was pulled back, except for some unruly curls circling her face. How could anyone look this good this early in the morning? It made him wonder how beautiful she'd be to wake up to— He quickly turned his wayward thoughts back to the supplier on the phone.

"Sure," he replied. "As long as they're here tomorrow first thing in the morning?" Lafe nodded when the man agreed. "Okay, thanks." He hung up the phone and gazed at Michelle.

He smiled. "Good morning."

"'Morning, Lafe," she answered.

Lafe tried to make contact with her elusive eyes, but he could tell she was embarrassed after Friday night. He got up. "How was your weekend?"

"It was fine."

Lafe grinned and came toward her. "Good! I had a great time Friday night."

Michelle finally looked at him. "So did I . . . and so did T.J."

She chewed nervously on her lip. "But I feel it would be best if we keep things focused on business."

"I'm sorry you feel that way, because I enjoyed spending time with you and your son." He leaned closer. "I especially enjoyed kissing you."

Michelle sucked in a breath. "But it shouldn't have happened. And I had no right to dump my problems on you."

Lafe tried to hide his disappointment. He had hoped that she had changed her mind. He shrugged. "We're friends, Michelle. You needed to talk with someone."

Michelle had never shared the truth about her marriage with anyone. She'd only told Betty enough to satisfy her curiosity. It would have been better if she had never mentioned Tom at all. The last thing she wanted from Lafe was pity. "Look, I'd really appreciate it if...if you didn't say anything about what...what I told you."

"Michelle, I don't make jokes about other people's pain."

She couldn't miss the hurt she saw on his face, and she hurried to say, "I know, Lafe, and I'm sorry I said anything."

There was an uneasy silence in the room for a long time. Finally Lafe spoke. "How's T.J.?"

"He's fine," she said. She didn't want Lafe to know that her son had spent the entire weekend talking about "Lafe this, and Lafe that." "He can't wait for school to get out. The only way I can keep him focused is threatening not to let him play baseball."

"I think that would do it."

Lafe grinned and Michelle felt a ripple of excitement rush though her.

"Well, so far he's followed the rules. So I promised I would ask if you'd like to come...to one of his Little League games. He's not very good—this is his first year..."

"I'd love to," Lafe answered.

Michelle's eyes widened. "You would?"

Just then the trailer door swung open and Jeff walked in as Lafe said, "Just tell me when you want me."

The sandy-haired foreman looked embarrassed. "Excuse me. I'll come back later."

Lafe laughed and Michelle's cheeks reddened. "No, it's not what you think," she quickly said. "I mean...Lafe is just going to my son's ball game." Oh, brother. Now the whole crew would think there was something going on between her and Lafe.

Jeff just smiled as he turned to Lafe. "Here are the receipts for the supplies that were just delivered." He held out the copies. "It was short again."

Michelle intercepted the sheets. "What do you mean 'short again'?" She eyed the yellow paper. "This has happened before?"

"We've had a slight problem," Lafe said as he walked around the desk and sat down in the chair. "But nothing I couldn't handle."

"I should have been informed about this," Michelle said in her most authoritative voice. Why had Lafe kept it from her? Did he think she couldn't handle her job? "It's the project manager's job to be kept abreast of any and all problems on the site. I also pay the bills. Your job is to handle the subcontractors and make sure they honor their contracts to build the custom houses."

"I know what my job is," Lafe informed her, his anger flaring. "And I had planned to tell you about the shortage. Jeff just jumped the gun." He glanced at his foreman, then back at her. "Besides, it was cleared up with a phone call to the supplier."

"But it's happened again." She stood her ground and waved the paper in the air. "So it wasn't handled."

"Okay, then you handle it," Lafe challenged, hands on his hips.

"Okay, I will." *Well, that went pretty smoothly.* She ignored the slight tremble in her hands. She picked up her briefcase and started for the door.

"Why go all the way back to the office? Just work here," Lafe suggested. "The trailer is big enough. Besides, it will be better for both of us."

I don't think so, Michelle thought in panic, wanting to exit the small room. "But all my files . . ."

"I have the same invoices. And also all the supply sheets, which I planned to fax you today. So why not work here and then you can ask me about anything you don't understand."

Lafe got up from his desk, wondering if she would stick around or run. He saw her big doe eyes widen as if she had been trapped in a car's headlights. She looked vulnerable and confused. Hell! It served her right. Michelle had had him confused since the moment they'd met.

"Sure... Why not?" She shrugged and looked around the cluttered trailer for a place to work.

"Here, you can use this desk." Jeff walked over to a small table in the corner. He began clearing away papers and blueprints. After the surface was revealed, Jeff guided her to the chair and moved the phone so she could reach it. He pointed out how to use the copy and fax machines, then showed her to the coffeepot and got her a clean mug, warning her about Lafe's strong brew. He even sharpened a few pencils before leaving the trailer.

Now she sat across the small room from the man with broad shoulders and lean hips encased in snug-fitting jeans. And she was supposed to work. Ha! Lafe looked up as he talked on the phone, and smiled. Michelle wanted to throw something at him. How was she going to get Mr. Dynamite Green Eyes to go out and work so she could concentrate on her job?

Lafe held back a groan as he glanced toward Michelle. She would never know how innocently seductive she was just sitting there twisting her hair around her finger. "Do you need help with anything?"

"No!" Michelle lifted her hand. "I'm just going to make a few calls. I don't want this supplier to think he can get away with cutting our order. I'll just refuse to give him any more of our business."

Lafe saw her determination. It reminded him a lot of himself a few years ago. "Michelle, why don't you find out first why the order was short. Maybe he has a good reason—"

"We can't afford these kinds of holdups."

"Michelle...it will be another week before we need those beams. The crew has plenty to do as it is."

"But that's not the point—"

"It's exactly the point," he said, standing. "You're getting worked up over something that isn't important right now. Save your energy for when it's really needed."

Michelle knew Lafe was right. She didn't need to raise her stress level until she at least found out the problem. She picked up the phone and dialed the supplier's number. A few minutes later she discovered the problem. After she hung up, she glanced over at Lafe at his desk. To her surprise, he'd been watching her.

"Mr. Cochran apologized for the inconvenience. There was a mix-up at the lumberyard. You were right...." She lifted her chin stubbornly to shield herself from his reprimand. When it didn't come she went on to explain, "The owner's wife had been in a car accident. But he promised to have the rest delivered by eight o'clock tomorrow," she finished, bracing herself for at least the "I told you so."

"Glad you could work something out" was all Lafe said, then he left to check on the crew.

Michelle was alone for most of the day. Jeff returned with a sandwich for her. She thanked him, then continued to work, going over the cost sheets. So far, everything seemed to be going fine, but she wasn't going to get optimistic until the project was completed. Too many things could go wrong.

Around four-thirty Lafe returned to the office, announcing that they were finished for the day. Michelle disagreed, telling him that she had more work to do.

"Take care of it tomorrow. You're welcome to work out here."

"I just need another hour tonight."

Lafe shook his head. "Sorry, the office is closed."

"You can't do that."

"Try me, Michelle. Now, go home to T.J."

Michelle glared at him. After her marriage to Tom, she promised herself that no one was going to dictate to her.

"We can stand here and stare at each other, but I'm not in the mood," Lafe told her. "I'll just carry you out."

"You wouldn't dare."

He tossed her a challenging smile. "Oh, Michelle, don't ever dare me to do anything. You might be sorry."

Chapter Six

Michelle couldn't believe her ears. "You want me to do what?" she said into the phone, asking Betty to repeat herself.

"I want you to dress in some jeans and a pair of boots so we can go out and celebrate your birthday."

Michelle rolled her eyes. "Betty... I'd rather not. I have too much work to do. Anyway, I'm past the age where I want to celebrate turning another year older."

"Hey, it's not every day your best friend turns thirty. We can't let it go by without doing something. What time should I pick you up?"

Michelle knew she had lost the argument, so she might as well give in. "Don't make it before eight. I have a lot of work to finish before I can go anywhere."

"I hope my father realizes what a dedicated employee you are."

"If he doesn't, I'm sure you'll remind him."

"I think he knows." Betty added, "Call Margaret and tell her that I'll pick up T.J. so he can spend the night with Billy. Then I'll come by for you."

"All right, see you later. Oh, Betty—wait," she called into the phone.

"What?"

"Thanks for remembering my birthday." Michelle sighed.

"Hey—you'd do the same for me. See you later."

About nine o'clock Michelle climbed out of Betty's car, realizing she never should have let her friend talk her into this. She looked down at the black, pointed-toe cowboy boots Betty had borrowed for her. Michelle had also been loaned a rose-colored western blouse and black jeans. All she needed was the hat to complete the outfit.

"Betty, I don't know about this," Michelle began. "These jeans are awfully tight. I don't think I can breathe."

Betty walked around her late-model sedan. "You don't need to breathe or sit down. You're going to be dancing all night," she promised as she slipped her arm through her friend's and headed toward the large building called the Cactus Saloon.

Michelle had heard the girls in the office talking about the country-and-western dance club. It was notorious for having plenty of good-looking guys. Oh, boy, she thought, taking a calming breath. She hadn't been to a bar in years, and never without Tom. The twangy sound of the band singing country music greeted them as they stepped through the double doors.

Michelle took a moment to adjust to the dimly-lit room as Betty shot off toward the back of the large club. She seemed to know exactly where she was going. Betty had always marched to her own tune. Michelle envied her for that. She also envied her friend for her long legs, since she had trouble keeping up. Finally Betty stopped at a group of tables decorated with colorful balloons, around which stood a lot of familiar people. Michelle froze. Oh, wonderful! A surprise party.

Blushing, Michelle managed a smile as she searched the faces. Her friends from the office were all in attendance, including Ben and his wife, Mary, Peggy and even Chris

Lawson. The good-looking blonde was the first to wish her a happy birthday and give her a kiss on the cheek.

Michelle laughed, then stepped back from his embrace.

Chris frowned. "What's so funny?"

"All the women in the office will be jealous." She spoke into his ear to be heard over the music.

"You're always saying that—just who are these women?"

"Stop by and see me tomorrow, I'll give you the list."

While Michelle talked with her guests, someone handed her a glass of wine. She took a few sips as her gaze traveled through the large crowd. She was fascinated by the couples moving in a circular motion around the dance floor.

"It's not as difficult as it looks."

Michelle immediately recognized Lafe's voice and turned around to find him standing next to her. He was wearing black jeans and shiny boots, highlighted perfectly by a light-colored western shirt and a black hat. He made every other man in the place fade in comparison. She groaned inwardly, realizing she was having trouble breathing, and it wasn't because of her jeans. It was because of his.

"Lafe. I didn't expect you to be here. Of course, I didn't expect anyone to be here." She laughed nervously.

Michelle really hadn't expected to see him tonight. It had been last Thursday since she'd seen or talked to him. Friday afternoon she'd called him with a problem and was told by Jeff that he was unable to reach him.

"I didn't want to miss the chance to wish you a happy birthday." He lowered his head and placed a soft kiss on her cheek.

Michelle blushed, but that didn't stop her from wanting more.

Suddenly the music slowed and Lafe took Michelle's hand in his. "C'mon, let's dance."

"But I don't think... It's not a good idea." It was the truth; she hadn't danced since high school. Besides, she didn't need to get anywhere near this man.

"It's a great idea. I get to hold you." He walked her to the floor. "Just follow my lead." He slipped his arm around her waist and drew her against him, resting his cheek on her hair.

Lafe moved with the beat of the soft ballad, aching to pull Michelle closer. He was surprised he'd gotten her to the floor so easily.

Oh, Michelle! Do you remember the last time I held you in my arms? he thought, bravely pressing her shapely body closer still. When he felt her slight tremble, he nearly lost control, but managed to keep his feet moving in rhythm to the music. Then all too soon the song ended. He moved back reluctantly, only raising his head a little to make contact with her bedroom eyes.

"That was nice," he managed in a hoarse voice.

Michelle held his gaze. "You're a good dancer."

Lafe shrugged. "I learned mostly while I was on the rodeo circuit."

"Do girls like cowboys who dance?" she asked, fighting a smile.

"I don't know—you tell me," Lafe challenged as the music started up again. He went to take her in his arms, when someone tapped him on the shoulder.

"Excuse me, but you can't hog the birthday girl."

They both turned to find a grinning Chris Lawson. Lafe wanted to push his fist right into the middle of the man's perfect set of teeth. Instead he stepped aside and allowed him to steal Michelle away.

Two hours later Lafe stood against the railing, nursing his second beer, watching Michelle waltz around the floor with partner after partner. She would throw her head back and laugh in that cute way of hers, making a man feel like tossing her over his shoulder and carrying her off. Lafe had no doubt that nearly every man Michelle had danced with that night felt that way about her, including him.

Damn! He'd tried everything to get her out of his system. He'd stayed away from her the past two weeks since he had taken them to the Angels game. He had even flown to the ranch last weekend and had dug postholes until his shoulders and back ached, but he still couldn't stop thinking about her. And she had made it clear that she wanted nothing but a business relationship. But he decided that wasn't going to stop him. Lafe wanted her. He glanced at Michelle once again. Wanted her more than any woman he had ever known. He just had to persuade her that he had serious courtship in mind.

The music stopped, and as if he had willed it, Michelle glanced his way. Then their eyes locked, and he suddenly felt his pulse leap with excitement. He wanted nothing more than to march out on the floor and claim Michelle as his.

Instead he took a last pull on his beer and set the bottle down on the table. He raised his hand to the brim of his hat and gave her a nod, then turned and walked away.

Michelle watched as Lafe disappeared through the crowd, and fought the urge to run after him. As much as she had been protesting any personal relationship, she had this strange sinking feeling in her stomach, as if he were deserting her.

Suddenly Betty appeared at Michelle's side. "C'mon, it's time for cake and opening your presents." Her best friend took her by the hand and led her back to the table were everyone was waiting, including her brother, Joe.

"Happy birthday, sis," he said, and kissed her on the cheek. "Sorry I was so late. Had a job to finish at the shop."

Michelle smiled. "I'm glad you could come." She really was. Glancing around the table at her friends, she realized how much she'd needed this.

With strong encouragement from the partyers, Michelle began opening her gifts. She unwrapped some pretty floral-trimmed stationery, a multicolored scarf and an expensive five-pound box of chocolates. To her surprise her brother gave her a bottle of her favorite perfume. With trembling hands, she opened the small package to find a necklace. There was an admiring gasp from the women at the party when she held up the gold chain adorned with a delicate shamrock charm.

Michelle tried to make light of Lafe's gift, but she knew it was more personal than she would have liked. Why couldn't he just have gotten her flowers? She could just hear the gossip in the office tomorrow morning. Stories of her party would be all over the building. Thank you, Lafe Colter.

Lafe sat at his desk, studying the flowery stationery. For the past thirty minutes, he'd read and reread the short note Michelle had sent him, trying to hide his disappointment that she hadn't thanked him for the necklace in person. Instead she had written him an impersonal note and had it delivered to the site along with the project mail. He found himself wanting her to take the time and come out herself. He hadn't seen or heard from her in three days, not since the party.

Oh, she had been at the site doing her job, all right, but she'd somehow managed to arrive after he'd left to go see the architect or talk with the building inspector.

Jeff came into the trailer. "Hey, boss. We got the sample tile delivery for the model, but it's different. They said the color we want is discontinued." The foreman handed Lafe the invoice. "Want me to call them?"

Lafe frowned as he examined the order. Damn! He didn't want this headache. They had been on schedule, then Ben had decided he wanted the work speeded up on the model home. "How far off is it?"

"It's more a green than a blue."

"Call the decorator and see if she can adjust," Lafe said, but when Jeff started across the room, he added, "Make sure she knows that it will probably take another month to get the reorder."

"Should I call Michelle, too?"

Lafe found he'd like nothing more than to see her, not especially for business reasons, either. "First let's find out what the interior decorator wants to do."

Jeff gave Lafe a funny look. "Is there something the matter between you and Michelle? I mean, normally you hand everything over to the project manager, especially the problems."

Lafe shrugged. "I guess I'm getting charitable in my old age."

The foreman grinned. "Maybe you're trying to make points with the pretty project manager."

Lafe ignored his comment. Although they were friends and had worked together for the past five years, Lafe tried hard to keep his personal life private.

"You're not at all actin' like the love 'em and leave 'em guy I used to know." Jeff cocked an eyebrow. "It seems to me that one dark-haired lady has you tied up in knots."

Lafe jerked his head up to deny it, but realized that what his foreman had said was true. "Why don't we just get back to business? Call the decorator and see what she has to say. I'll talk to Michelle later."

"Talk to me later about what?"

They both turned to find the door open and Michelle standing there. She was dressed for the site in a pair of jeans and boots.

"Just a small problem..." Jeff started to say, but stopped when Lafe raised his hand.

"Hello, Michelle." Lafe tried to act casual, but he was remembering the last time he'd seen her...when he'd held her in his arms. Suddenly there didn't seem to be enough air in his lungs.

"What problem?" she repeated.

"Jeff was just going to call the decorator," Lafe began. "The sample tiles came in today. The color we ordered for the model is discontinued."

He watched as Michelle's cheery expression disappeared.

"How long to replace it?" she asked.

"Since it's custom..." Lafe pursed his lips. "Probably three to fours weeks."

"Darn it, they were supposed to be a reliable company." She began to pace. "The salesman promised—"

"It happens sometimes," he interrupted. "I'm not saying it's right, but in this business it's more the norm. So we either choose from the samples we have or hold up everything and reorder through another manufacturer. That might cost us a lot of time and money."

"I know that," she snapped, then looked at Jeff apologetically. Lafe knew this had been about the third thing that had gone wrong this week. And with Ben wanting to speed up the work on the model . . .

Lafe grabbed a couple of hard hats. "Jeff, call the decorator and set up a meeting for later," he said as he took hold of Michelle's arm. "C'mon, let's go for a walk." He felt her resistance, but kept tugging her along until they were out of the trailer.

"Look, Lafe, I don't have time to go for a walk." Michelle pulled from his grasp.

"I think we both could used a little open space." He set the hard hat on her head. "Sometimes it helps when you're trying to solve a problem."

The cool breeze whipped Michelle's hair in her face and she brushed it back as they walked toward the bluff. She had acted unprofessionally. She had to pull herself together, stop worrying about running into Lafe all the time and just do her job.

"Sorry, I guess I let my temper get the best of me. But I was so careful about all the suppliers."

Lafe smiled as they continued through the high grass. "Hey, you just care about the project," he said. "Too bad you don't care about yourself as much."

"I care about me."

"Do you? How about the long hours you put in?"

Michelle knew that in her line of work, women had to work twice as hard as men to prove themselves. This was a male-dominated field. And someone like Lafe Colter would never understand how much courage it took for her to stand up for herself. Over the past year and a half, working for Stafford Investments had been more than a job, and she had gained confidence and self-esteem. "This is an important project," she said.

Lafe raised a calming hand. "I know, but that's all it is. A project." His eyes grew intense. "Michelle, don't let your work end up being the only thing in your life. You have T.J. He's what's really important."

Michelle clenched her fists, holding back her anger. She didn't need anyone telling her that her son was important.

She would like to cut back her hours to be there for him. "So is supporting him," she protested.

Lafe looked abashed by her reply. "You're right. I'm sorry. I...I had no right to butt into your private life. You're doing a fine job with him."

As Lafe started back to the site, Michelle reached out and touched his arm. "No, Lafe, wait. I'm the one who should apologize. I'm being overly sensitive. But I'm the project manager and I don't want anything kept from me. I just want to do *my* job." And now was not the time to bring up her trouble with the crew. Some of them had decided early on that they didn't like working for a woman. Luckily there only seemed to be a few troublemakers.

"I wasn't keeping anything from you, Michelle." Lafe pulled back, causing her to release his arm. "I planned to tell you. But I haven't seen you since last week."

"I've been here," she countered. Michelle had been at the site, just not when Lafe was. In fact, she had worked all of Saturday morning, going over invoices. "And even if I'm not here, I'm usually at the office. Only a phone call away."

She studied Lafe's handsome face, the way his dark hair curled around the rim of his hard hat. She tried desperately to forget what it felt like to be held in his arms, to not want to be there again.

"I think you need to be here every day," Lafe said. "Preferably when I'm here. That is, if you want to keep on top of any problems that might come up."

His words seemed more like a challenge than a request. Michelle was enough of a professional to know that avoiding him wasn't going to get the job done. "I'll be by first thing in the morning—every morning. I, too, think it's important that we're able to reach each other—at all times." Just where were you last weekend Mr. Colter? she wanted to demand.

"That might not be possible, but I'm usually here during working hours. And Jeff is available to handle things."

It wasn't a perfect plan, but at least they'd agreed to deal more directly with each other. Michelle had to face the fact that Lafe was going to be a part of her life for the next few months. "I agree Jeff is capable."

Lafe nodded. "And I agree to let you do your job without any interference from me. We'll talk out everything that has to do with the project, so we both know what's going on."

"Good," Michelle said amiably, not wanting Lafe to know that some of the men weren't exactly crazy about the idea of a woman being boss. But she wanted to handle that difficulty her way. Besides, it was a personal problem between her and the men. It had nothing to do with business or Lafe.

At the quiet neighborhood park, Michelle sat anxiously on the bleachers, waiting for her son's baseball game to start. The entire Donovan family was in attendance—her father, brothers, Joe and Pat, and Pat's wife, Cathy, and their four-year-old daughter, Amy. All waiting to cheer T.J.'s team to victory.

Looking around the park once again, Michelle wondered if Lafe would show. Of course, he could be held up by the traffic, she thought hopefully, knowing his coming wasn't a good idea. During the past week they had managed to work together, and not once had he stepped over that professional line. About as close as they had gotten was sharing a sandwich at lunch. The last thing she wanted was for Lafe Colter to think one Little League ball game would change that.

"It's only a game, honey," Michael Donovan said as he patted his daughter's hand.

Michelle smiled. "I know, Dad. I guess I'm a little nervous. T.J. has practiced so hard."

She had always thought her father a handsome man, with his thick, wavy gray hair, sparkling blue eyes and slight Irish brogue. He'd lost his wife twenty-five years ago, and had concentrated on raising his three children. But he could still charm the ladies.

"He'll do just fine," her father reassured her.

Just then Michelle caught sight of Lafe standing beside the dugout, talking with T.J. Their conversation lasted a few minutes, then Lafe held up his hand and her son gave him a high five. Her heart began to pound rapidly when Lafe strolled toward the bleachers. He was dressed in his usual jeans and western shirt, and a pair of scuffed boots. Lafe caught sight of her and started to climb through the crowd to the top. She followed his movement up the rows of seats, along with every other admiring female in the stands.

"Hi, Michelle." He took the seat next to her, as if she had saved the spot especially for him.

She managed a nod, but when she tried to talk her throat was suddenly too dry. Luckily Joe took care of the introductions to the rest of the family. Lafe stood up and shook her father's and brothers' hands.

"I'm sorry I'm late. There was an accident on the freeway," he explained as he returned to his seat.

His green eyes gazed into hers for a second, then he was distracted by a question from Joe. Michelle's sister-in-law flashed her a sign of approval.

"You look a little nervous, Mom," Lafe teased.

Michelle watched her son wave from the dugout, then run out to the outfield to start the game. "I'm just a little worried about T.J."

There was no score in the first inning. It wasn't until the second that the other team scored three runs. But T.J.'s team, the Giants, scored four in the next inning. Michelle's heart sank into her stomach when T.J. came up to bat and swung twice at the baseball tee and missed. Then her son stepped back from the plate, rubbed some dirt between his hands and glanced up at the bleachers. At first Michelle thought he was looking for her, but then realized it was Lafe. They exchanged a thumbs-up sign and T.J. walked back into the batter's box. This time he hit the ball and it went sailing past the second baseman. The crowd cheered as T.J. ran to first base.

Almost two hours later the game ended and the Giants won, eight to five. T.J. ran to the bleachers, happily accepting the praise of his family. Then he turned to Lafe.

"Hey, Lafe, did you see my hit in the fifth?"

Lafe grinned. "Sure did."

Michelle interrupted her son's play by play. "Everyone back to the house for a victory barbecue. We're having ribs with the Donovans' special sauce," she announced.

Joe made a whooping sound and swung his niece around in a circle.

Michelle smiled as her son tugged on her arm. "What, honey?"

"Mom, can Lafe come for ribs, too?"

Michelle felt her cheeks flame. Oh, God! She had forgotten about Lafe. She stole a glance at the outsider standing in the midst of her family. He tried to look cool and uncaring, but Michelle sensed his loneliness. She couldn't turn this man away, for anything.

"Of course... Lafe can come to the barbecue."

Michelle ended up driving home by herself, since T.J. wanted to ride with Lafe. Everyone arrived at the house in minutes, since the field was only a few blocks away. The men and children disappeared into the backyard, while Cathy and Michelle organized things in the kitchen.

"Here, let's take some beer and soda out to the patio," Michelle suggested as she rearranged things in the refrigerator.

"Lafe seems like a nice guy," Cathy said out of the blue.

Michelle looked at her pretty, brunette sister-in-law. They hadn't been close through the years—but lately they had made up for lost time. Michelle loved her like a sister.

"Yes, he is a nice man to work with." She picked up the beers and headed for the patio.

Joining the men out in the backyard, she looked around and saw Pat trying to start the grill. Her brother Joe was talking to Lafe about ranching, with T.J. sitting close by, listening intently. When she handed out the beers, Lafe scooted over, giving her room to sit down at the table. Michelle knew she had no choice and took her spot on the bench. Her bare thigh brushed Lafe's rough jeans more than once, but that didn't seem to bother him. Well, it was driving Michelle crazy. She was relieved when T.J. asked for something to eat.

Returning to the kitchen for their snack, she grabbed the bag of pretzels on the counter. When she turned around she discovered Lafe had followed her inside. She jumped, her hand covering her heart. "Oh—you scared me."

"Sorry, I didn't mean to."

He smiled, and Michelle felt her legs go all rubbery, so much so that she had to lean against the cabinet for support. When he moved closer, she swallowed anxiously, hearing her family's voices outside the kitchen window. At any moment someone could walk in, but when he reached out and cupped her cheeks, she didn't protest. Not even when his mouth came down to meet hers.

The touch of his lips was soft, tender, as he caressed her mouth. Then, as if what was happening were a dream, he slowly broke off the kiss. Taking a breath, Michelle looked up to see Lafe's mesmerizing green eyes. She blinked and tried to regain her composure. This time when she glanced at his face he smiled and touched the charm hanging around her neck.

"I'm glad you like your present." He winked, then took the pretzels from her and left.

Angry with her reaction to the kiss, Michelle took a few moments to calm herself. She opened a bag of chips and poured them into a bowl. Why couldn't things be left as they were—strictly business? But was that the way she really wanted it? she wondered as her head replayed the feel of Lafe's mouth on hers. A shiver ran through her body. It didn't matter what she thought; she wasn't going to get involved with the man.

With new determination, Michelle pulled the ribs out of the refrigerator. She pulled down the plates and got out the flatware. The sooner she had the food on the table the sooner she could send Mr. Colter home.

She carried the platter out to the patio and handed it to her brother. "How's the fire coming, Pat? We need to get this show on the road."

Michelle felt Lafe's eyes on her, but refused to give him the satisfaction of even glancing his way. She had to keep her focus on preparing the meal, she told herself as she headed back to the kitchen for the rest of the food.

The barbecue ribs were a big hit, and so was Cathy's potato salad. Everything disappeared as it usually did around the Donovan family. Lafe showed no shyness as he followed the other men and went after a second helping. T.J. and his cousin, Amy, finished their dinner and retreated to the family room to watch TV.

The party broke up about ten when Pat and Cathy gathered up their sleepy daughter from the den and carried her to the car. Her father had already left so he could get some rest to go fishing at dawn. Michelle glanced out the kitchen window to find Lafe and Joe folding chairs and cleaning up.

Michelle called into the den, "T.J., it's time for bed."

"Ah, Mom."

"C'mon, say good-night to everyone."

Joe and Lafe were joking as they entered the house. It was as if they had been friends for years. "Everything is put away and I locked the patio door," Joe told her, then turned to his nephew. "Hey, T.J., you still up?"

The boy frowned, casting a sideways glance at his mother. "Not for long."

"Sounds like a good idea. That's just where I'm headed right now." He kissed his sister and T.J. "Six o'clock comes awfully early. Lafe, nice seeing you again." Joe shook his hand. "I hope we can do this again soon."

"I'd like that," Lafe concurred as he accepted Joe's hand.

"Good." Joe waved and was out the door.

There were a few moments of awkward silence. Michelle hoped that Lafe would say his goodbye and follow her brother out the door. He didn't, and finally Michelle coaxed her son toward his bedroom. "No more stalling, son. It's time for bed."

"Can I show Lafe something in my bedroom?"

Michelle rolled her eyes. She didn't need this. "Honey, it's late. Lafe has to go to work early...."

"I can take ten minutes to see T.J.'s toys," Lafe said, studying her reaction before turning to the boy. "But by then you'll be tucked in your bunk, pretending you're sleeping under the stars."

"Wow! Really?"

"Really." Lafe took T.J.'s hand and walked with him down the hall.

Lafe turned on the light in the bedroom. He came inside and sat down on the twin bed covered with the cowboy comforter. Lafe talked the boy out of dragging out his baseball cards and other little-boy treasures. Instead he persuaded him to get ready for bed. Lafe knew that Michelle wasn't very happy at the moment, and he'd be pushing his luck if he kept T.J. up later than the allotted time.

"I'm glad you came to my ball game," T.J. began as he finished putting on his pj's. "All the guys get to have their fathers there and it was like I had a dad...." The boy's words faded out.

Lafe had no trouble identifying with the child. "Well, you had a lot of family there tonight—your grandfather, your mom and two uncles, an aunt and a cousin. I never knew my grandfather, and I had only one uncle." And his Uncle Ray would never have wasted time on a stupid kids' ball game, Lafe added silently.

T.J. climbed into bed. "I know, but I'm still glad you came." This time the boy didn't wait for an invitation to wrap his arms around Lafe, and hugged him tight.

Lafe was glad someone was happy. He recalled Michelle's surprised look when T.J. had invited him to stay for the barbecue. He could try to tell himself it didn't matter, but it did. Since he had never belonged to a family, he'd always felt awkward at family gatherings.

Lafe's throat closed up. "Anytime," he managed to whisper.

Chapter Seven

Michelle and Jeff walked through the first floor of the nearly completed model, going over her punch list. She already had several minor things written down that needed to be redone, and the foreman agreed to make sure they were brought up to the architect's specs in time for the open house.

They were headed for the stairs, when Jeff's pager went off. With a frustrating groan, he pulled the device off his belt. "You go on. I'll catch up after I make a quick phone call," he said, and took off toward the cellular phone on the counter.

Michelle didn't hesitate as she climbed the beautiful wood-carved staircase, admiring the detailed work. The carpentry on the whole had been top-notch. But once she reached the second floor she could tell that the baseboards and the molding around the doors weren't the same grade of wood as downstairs.

Michelle knew she was going to take flak for complaining, especially from the two carpenters. Bill and Larry had already voiced their opinions several times, mostly about her trying to do a man's job. She had heard many hurtful comments since starting Ocean Bluff. Everything from being called the "Dragon Lady" to remarks about her having PMS. Still, Michelle knew she couldn't let up now. Although she wanted the men's respect, she knew her job came first.

She caught up with the two workers. "Bill, Larry, I'd like to talk with you." She stopped outside the master bedroom. Larry was doing the molding around the doorjamb, and his partner was at the other bedroom door, doing the same. Michelle took a deep breath to hold her temper, realizing that they were using fir, not white oak, as requested on her sheet. Worst of all, they were ignoring her.

"I asked if I could talk with you both," she said in her best authoritative voice, but she felt her nervousness growing. She hated confrontation. Tom had never passed up the chance to use intimidation as a way of controlling her.

They stopped and exchanged glances, before Bill wandered over to her. He was a burly man, wearing a faded pocketed T-shirt that hugged his oversize belly. A carpenter's belt hung loosely around his low-riding Levi's. "Yeah. What do you want?"

"You're using the wrong grade of wood on the moldings and doorjambs. It doesn't meet with the architect's specs." She thumbed through her papers and came up with the correct grade and showed it to the indifferent carpenter.

"That's just for the first floor," Bill spoke up as he glanced up at the doorjamb. He shrugged. "This here's standard for bedrooms."

Michelle didn't much care for these two. They had been nothing but trouble since the beginning, and had done most of the complaining about her. She was just glad that Lafe was the contractor and he had to deal with them the majority of the time. She drew a deep breath, finding the strength not to back down. "That's not good enough. The specs that Lafe and I have call for white oak, first and *second* floor."

That got Larry's attention. "Lady, you can't mean that." He placed his hands on his hips and glared at her. "Do you know how much that's gonna cost?"

"I'm sorry, but until it's done correctly there won't be a check released, to you or your contractor," she countered, feeling her insides twisting. She couldn't let these men intimidate her from doing her job. "I'll give you till the end of the week to replace it."

Michelle knew that this was cutting it close, especially since Ben had planned the open house for the following weekend. That only gave her a little over twelve days. She made a note to recheck the molding and looked up from her clipboard. "And if you can't get the work done by then I'll have to back-charge you," Michelle finished. If looks could kill, she knew T.J. would be an orphan right now.

"Yes, sir, boss," Larry said with a mock salute.

Michelle turned and started down the hall, hearing some murmurs about her unfavorable ancestry. She just kept walking, knowing that if Lafe had done the same thing, the men wouldn't even have argued.

Jeff came up the stairs and rushed toward her. "Sorry it took so long, Michelle. Did you run into any problems?" the foreman asked.

Michelle smiled proudly. "No, nothing I couldn't handle."

"All right, I'll take care of it," Lafe said into the phone. "I know." He nodded and leaned back in his chair, listening to the complaint about Michelle. "Mrs. Royer is right about the materials. They weren't what we agreed on. So you'd better get them replaced before the week is out, or you'll be formally written up. And I don't think you'll want to lose future jobs with Stafford Investments." Lafe didn't wait to hear any more and slammed the receiver down.

Lafe pushed out of his seat. "What did that guy think he was doing, trying to get away with using substandard materials? Michelle was clearly in the right to make him replace it."

He combed his fingers through his hair. Damn! He was letting himself get so worked up over this job, he was talking to himself. Or was he worked up because of the way some of the crew were treating Michelle?

Either way he needed a break for a while. And he was going to take one. He was planning on flying to the ranch for the weekend. It would be his last chance to get away before the open house in ten days. And after that there wouldn't be any peace; people would be all over the site.

Besides, Michelle was driving him crazy with her feelings running hot and cold. The night of the barbecue, she'd acted as though she'd wanted the kiss he'd stolen in the kitchen, but a few hours later, coming out of T.J.'s room, it was as if she didn't want anything to do with him. So he had gone home. Fine. He didn't stick around where he wasn't wanted. It didn't matter anyway; in a few months he was moving on.

The past few weeks, he'd only seen Michelle around the site during the early morning. But she had always been too busy to spend much time with him. If he even acted as though he wanted to get personal she found an excuse to leave. Although most of the crew had handled her being in charge, he still had gotten complaints from a few of the diehards who didn't like taking orders from a woman. Lafe had known that Michelle was pushing to do a good job. He also knew the construction business was a tough field for women. It had even taken him a few years to get used to the idea that a woman could handle the job.

Lafe smiled, remembering the first woman he'd ever hired, Mary Elizabeth Murphy. Bess had been nearly as small as Michelle was. And although she had learned her trade well from her five elder brothers and was licensed, no one would hire her. Lafe had taken a chance that day, and found it was one of the best decisions he'd ever made. He only wished she had been able to travel to California and work on Ocean Bluff.

His thoughts turned back to Michelle. Since she had come into his life, he hadn't been able to think clearly about anything. She'd been insistent that all she wanted was a business relationship, but he knew differently. When she was in his arms and returning his kisses, the last thing either one of them was thinking about was business. Michelle couldn't hide her response to him; she came alive in his arms. And just the thought of her stirred his body. Damn! He rubbed his hands over his face. Why couldn't he get her out of his mind?

Just then Jeff walked into the trailer. "They delivered the shipment of lumber." He handed Lafe the invoice.

"Good. Get the crew on the framing after lunch."

"Before you get too excited," Jeff continued, "I got a call earlier and it seems there's going to be a delay on the roofing materials."

Lafe remained calm. "How long?"

"Looks like about three weeks."

"What!" Lafe added up in his head the amount of time it took for framing and preparation. It would be cutting things close; if any delays came up they'd be in trouble. "Make a few calls and see if you can find a company that will guarantee delivery sooner."

Jeff nodded, but didn't go to the phone. "Before I start phoning, there's one more problem.

Lafe sighed as he sat down on the edge of his desk. He knew it had to be something big if Jeff was hesitating. "What is it?"

"Remember that shipment of bathroom fixtures we got two weeks ago?"

"Yeah, right now it seems to be the only thing that has come in on time and without a shortage," Lafe joked, only to release some tension.

"Well, that's how they arrived, but now there seems to be some missing."

"What?" Lafe wrinkled his brow. "You mean like stolen?"

Jeff nodded slowly.

"How can that be? We have security."

"I have a hunch it might be an inside job." Jeff raised his hand in defense. "But right now I have no proof."

Lafe hated not being able to trust his crew. "How much stuff is gone?"

"About a fourth of the bathroom fixtures. A few doorknobs, a few boxes of tile. All special orders—the expensive stuff. They seem to know where everything is, and until

I went looking no one noticed anything was gone. What do you want to do about it?''

The pounding in Lafe's temples intensified. He positively needed time at the ranch.

Michelle got out of her car Friday morning. Today was the day she had to recheck the carpenters' work. She only hoped that Larry and Bill had taken her seriously and made all the changes she'd asked for. Michelle smiled hopefully. Maybe this incident had been what she'd needed. With her refusal to back down, she'd let them know she meant business.

She picked up her briefcase, and on her way to the trailer, she took time to enjoy the crew at work. The framing was going great. No delays, thank God. She glanced over her shoulder at the Wedgwood blue-and-white, Cape Cod-style model, watching the landscapers grading the soil, soon to be a lush Bermuda tiff green lawn. The concrete circular driveway had been poured yesterday. She smiled. Everything was going to be gorgeous for the open house next weekend.

With renewed energy, Michelle jogged up the trailer steps and opened the door. She was anxious to get to work. She stopped dead in her tracks when she found Lafe stretched out on the sofa, sound asleep.

His stocking feet hung over one end. He was fully clothed in a blue denim shirt and jeans, and she couldn't stop herself from gazing at his perfect body: his broad chest, flat stomach, lean hips and long muscular legs. She studied his hands, resting against his waist, and recalled the strength, yet the gentleness, of his caresses. She felt a hot shiver run down her spine; it was as though someone had lit a match and set her afire.

Good heavens, girl. Pull yourself together, she chided. *You have a job to do. And so does Lafe.*

What was he doing asleep at eight in the morning? Maybe he'd had a late night. She had heard some of the crew talking about going out for happy hour after work. She listened to Lafe's even breathing and his dead-to-the world snore.

Michelle's temper flared. Well, he could just party on his own time. They had a project to finish. She marched to the sofa and not too gently jabbed him in the shoulder.

"Lafe! Get up," she ordered and immediately got a response.

"What? What?" he mumbled groggily. "What the..." He looked up at her. "Michelle, what's the matter?"

She folded her arms over her chest. "That's what I'd like to know. What are you doing asleep?"

Lafe was worthless without his first cup of coffee. Hell, he couldn't even focus. He managed to sit up, rubbing his eyes. "I didn't get any sleep last night." He watched as Michelle's body stiffened and her expression grew even angrier.

"Well, you can party all you want as far as I'm concerned," she began, "but I think it's very unprofessional when you aren't ready to work the next day."

Lafe gave her an disbelieving look. She thought he had been partying all night? He started to smile. And she was jealous. His smile turned into a full-fledged grin. "I made it to work."

"But in what condition? You're still half-asleep."

Lafe couldn't help but tease her. "I had a long night. C'mon, Michelle, give a guy a break."

She held back a gasp. "I can't believe you. How dare you ask..." She was stumbling over her words. "This project is important and if you can't do your job—"

"That's the reason I'm so tired—I was doing my job." He grabbed his work boots and began putting them on.

"Oh, yeah, sure."

"C'mon, Michelle, you're jumping to conclusions. Why not try a little trust?"

"I have my reasons," she said willfully. Yet he could see the hurt in her eyes.

Lafe stood and combed his hand through his messy hair. "All right, I was here all night, keeping guard." He walked to the coffeemaker to start a fresh pot. "We seem to have a thief in our midst."

"What?"

He glanced over his shoulder. "Someone has been stealing from us. Bathroom fixtures, brass doorknobs, some boxes of tile." Lafe grabbed a paper off his desk and handed it to Michelle. "Jeff took inventory yesterday and here's what we're missing."

Michelle's eyes widened. "How could this happen with security around?"

Lafe shrugged. "We're not sure. Either they're the ones doing the stealing, or they are allowing some of the men back on the site after-hours to take the supplies. Either way we stand to lose a lot of money if it keeps up. So Jeff and I stayed last night and took turns watching, hoping we'd catch someone. But no such luck."

Michelle hated hearing what was going on. She especially hated the fact that she hadn't been notified. "Why didn't you call me?"

Lafe sighed and went back to making coffee. "To be honest, we thought that if we caught them in the act you wouldn't have to worry about it."

She tried to hide her disappointment, but she'd never been very good at it. "It's my job to worry."

"But what could you have done? You couldn't drive out here and spend the night. No one expects you to."

"You did," she countered.

"I'm not a single parent with a seven-year-old son."

Michelle knew Lafe had a point, but she wasn't about to let him know. "Next time I want to be called."

She lifted her chin, meeting his challenging gaze head-on. She waited and waited, until he came closer and was looking down at her intensely. When he reached out and his warm hand cupped her cheek, her breathing came in shallow gasps.

"You know, Michelle, I can't tell you how many times I've fantasized about you and me spending the night together," he whispered in a husky voice.

Michelle closed her eyes as his warm breath caressed her face and she couldn't help but wonder if he was going to kiss her.

"But as you have suggested many times in the past, we shouldn't mix business with pleasure. And if we spent the night together it would definitely be pleasure...for both of us."

Michelle's eyes darted open to find Lafe's teasing grin, then he released her and crossed the room.

"Tell Jeff I'm gonna grab a quick shower. Be back in about an hour."

Michelle clenched her fists as Lafe strolled out the door, practically slamming it in her face. All the time she was thinking of ways to kill the man.

Over the next few hours, Michelle calmed down. She was done inspecting the carpenters' work, and was pleased with the results. They had changed all the moldings and baseboards, and the finished work was beautiful. The house was rapidly becoming a reality. The carpeting had been installed, and all the tiling was completed. There were just a few minor things left to do.

With clipboard in hand, Michelle began her trip through the dream house. The model was two stories, nearly forty-five-hundred square feet. All the homes were set on one-acre parcels, and six of the twelve models backed up against the bluff. And they all had access to a private stretch of beach below. Never in her life did Michelle expect to afford a home like this, but that didn't stop her from wanting one.

She climbed the stairs, running her hand along the oak banister. When she reached the top she headed for the master suite at the end of the long hall, in the opposite direction of the other three bedrooms. She walked into the huge room with a fireplace adorning one wall. The other wall was done all in glass, with a pair of French doors leading to a private balcony and the breathtaking view of the Pacific Ocean.

She made a note to talk with the interior decorator about the drapes, then moved on to the master bath, checking the tile work and fixtures in the double shower stall. They were perfect. The large sunken tub across the room under the skylight made Michelle's mouth water just thinking about stealing an hour of peace and quiet.

Reluctantly she moved on to her next destination, the spacious walk-in closets. She stepped inside to examine the special shelving the architect had requested. Suddenly the closet door slammed shut. It's only the wind, she thought, but when she tried the knob it wouldn't budge. She was locked in. How was that possible?

Don't panic, she had been telling herself for the past thirty minutes. The crew was at lunch, someone would be back soon to get her out. It wasn't as if she was being left for the night. All at once terror raced through her. She got off the floor and began to pound on the door once more.

"Hey, get me out of here!" she cried into the silence. "Somebody...." She felt tears and blinked them away. Damn! She didn't want to cry. She didn't want the men to see her this way. She swallowed hard and began to pound on the door again. "Hey, get me out."

"Michelle?"

She froze hearing the familiar voice. "Lafe, I'm in here," she called out, and heard the sound of something being moved away, then the doorknob turning. Within seconds the door opened and Lafe stood there. She didn't even think when she ran into his arms.

Lafe held on to Michelle, knowing she was having a tough time trying to stay composed. Being shut in wasn't much fun, joke or no joke. "You okay?"

Still not releasing her tight hold on him, she nodded. "I hate being closed in."

"I think everybody does." He ran his hand over her silky hair. "Practical jokes aren't funny sometimes, especially when you're on the receiving end."

Michelle raised her head with a incredulous look on her face. "What do you mean, practical jokes? The men ... the crew was in on this? Well, they can't do this." She pushed away from Lafe and headed for the door, but he grabbed her and held her back.

"Oh, no, you don't. You're not going to say one word to the men!"

She struggled for release, but Lafe held fast. "If you think they're going to get away with this, you're mistaken."

Lafe pulled the door shut again. He leaned against the doorjamb and folded his arms across his chest, as if daring her to try to get by. "Let's talk."

Michelle froze. "Lafe, get out of my way."

"We're not leaving this room until you calm down and promise not to set the men off again."

"Set the men off! They're the ones who shut me in here. All I want is for them to do their jobs."

"Michelle, if you want their respect, you have to give a little, too." He hated having to tell her that, but someone had to. "You've been riding some of the men pretty hard."

She turned around, her hands on her hips. "That's because they don't listen to what I say."

Lafe nodded. "I agree, some of the men don't like taking orders from a woman, but two-thirds of that crew out there have done a damn good job so far. Still, you have to get along with the *whole* crew."

The lighting in the closet was dim, but he saw her eyes tearing up and her hands clench into fists. She was trying to control both her anger and her fear.

Lafe wanted to take her in his arms, protect her from all the hurt. He pushed away from the doorjamb and went to her. "Michelle, let me help."

"Yeah, sure," she said, moving toward the opposite end of the closet. "You men all say you want to help. What you really want is control. And if we happen to have a little authority you have to find a way to belittle us—or, better yet, take it away."

"Dear God, Michelle! What did your husband do to you?"

Michelle's tears blinded her as panic like she'd never known welled in her throat. She felt so exposed...so naked. But she still fought pridefully. "Whatever happened in my marriage is no one's business."

"Well, I'm sure as hell making it mine," he growled, then turned and began to pace the small room. After a few seconds he spoke again. "Michelle, when you were in Colorado and came into my room, I thought . . . I thought it was because of the pain over your husband's death." He paused in front of her, but she remained silent.

"For nearly a year," Lafe continued, "I thought that was the reason you wanted to make love. Tell me, Michelle. Tell me that you didn't want me as a substitute for your husband." He gripped her shoulders and shook her gently. "Tell me you wanted *me* that night, not that . . . that bastard you were married to."

Michelle hated her vulnerability. "Okay, okay, it was you I wanted," she confessed as she shut her eyes. "I wanted to forget the years of pain and heartbreak. I wanted someone to hold me, make me feel alive, feel loved."

She glanced away as if to gather her courage, then began again. "When Tom died, I was almost relieved. Is that what you wanted to hear, Lafe? That my husband controlled me, my life, so that I couldn't even think for myself?" She swallowed back a sob. "God! If I tried to do anything on my own he ridiculed me, telling me I was stupid. And he made sure that I couldn't get along without him. He had me quit my job." Brushing a tear off her cheek, she moved to the far wall. "Oh, he used the excuse that I was pregnant. But after he sold my car, I wasn't even allowed to go to the grocery store without asking him."

Lafe wanted desperately to hit something. "Michelle, Tom was sick."

She looked resentful. "Don't you think I know that? I lived with him for ten years. I had been planning to leave him. Tom's rages were out of control, especially toward T.J. We had a big fight about it, and when he left you could hear the brakes squealing as he drove out of the neighborhood." She raised her eyes to meet Lafe's. "I'm the one who caused the accident. . . ."

"Michelle, you can't believe that." Now so many things made sense to him. Her iron will around the crew, her struggle to do everything herself. Her pushing him away.

Lafe took hold of her hand. He raised it to his lips, pressing a kiss against her knuckles. "Trust me, Michelle, Tom's problems weren't caused by you. And trust me when I say I'd die before I'd ever intentionally hurt you." He stepped closer, and when she didn't resist, he drew her into his arms. "Let me hold you, Michelle. Let me kiss away the pain."

He lifted her chin so he could read her dark eyes. She still looked like a frightened animal. "I promise I won't do anything you don't want me to." He lowered his head so that their lips were only inches apart. "Tell me, Michelle. Tell me you want me, too."

Michelle closed her eyes and swayed against him. Her only thoughts were of how wonderful his mouth would feel on hers. Swallowing her fears, she answered, "Yes, I want you...."

Lafe wasted no time reacting to her admission as he cupped her face in his hands. "That's what I've been hoping you'd say." He lowered his mouth to hers.

Michelle parted her lips to meet his. She felt his mouth touch hers briefly, then pull away. She groaned softly and felt his lips on hers again. There was no hesitation this time. Lafe's tongue entered her mouth, teasing and stroking, until soon she was responding eagerly.

Impatiently Michelle moved her hands to his chest, trying urgently to find the opening to his shirt. He shuddered when her fingers made contact with his warm skin. He tensed as her hands moved up to his neck and she threaded her fingers in his hair, deepening the kiss.

Lafe slowly tore his mouth away, trying to catch his breath. He nibbled on her neck as he crushed her body against his. "Oh, honey!" he groaned. "What are you doing to me?"

She sighed, feeling his lips against her skin, knowing she wasn't able to stand much more.

"Michelle, I want you so much." He took her mouth in another fierce kiss. He caressed her, then began tugging her blouse from the waistband of her jeans. Frustrated, he trailed his hands up the front of the blouse and cupped her breasts through the fabric. She trembled as she arched back, allowing him better access. He finally managed to undo a few buttons and reached inside, covering her breast with his hand.

"Lafe," she gasped as he caressed her nipple through the sheer bra until it grew hard against his rough fingers. Then he bent his head and used his mouth to drive her further out of her mind.

She felt herself being lowered to the plush carpeting, then Lafe's delicious weight pressing against her. She felt powerless to resist. It was as if she were being carried off on a sensual journey, as he teased her with a trail of hot kisses from her ear down her neck.

Lafe was breathless as he raised his head and looked down at her. He had never wanted any woman this much. "Do you know how beautiful you are?" He brushed away a few strands of hair that lay across her cheeks.

She gave him a shy look. "I'm glad you think so."

Lafe brought her back into his arms and kissed her. She was ready with parted lips to receive his hungry mouth. He groaned when Michelle's body arched against his, driving him closer to the edge.

"Oh, Lafe," she gasped.

"Michelle! Lafe!"

Jeff's voice interrupted them and they both froze.

Lafe was the first to move. He stood up and quickly straightened his clothes. Tucking in his shirt, he combed his fingers through his hair and went to the door. He looked outside the closet and found his foreman in the master suite. Lafe was as nervous as a teenager getting caught by his girlfriend's father.

"Hey, Jeff."

The foreman turned around and smiled. "I wondered where you were. Can't find Michelle, either."

"She's probably down at the bluff. I'm just finishing a shelf in here. Why don't I meet you back at the trailer—say, in fifteen minutes?"

Jeff studied the half-opened door. "I could help you here."

"No, I'm just about finished," Lafe argued. The last thing he wanted to do was embarrass Michelle. "You go on down. I'll be there in a few minutes."

Lafe watched Jeff nod and head out of the room, then he came back inside the closet, closing the door. He smiled as he looked down at Michelle, who was sitting on the floor.

"That was close." He chuckled as he reached for her. He wanted her back in his arms.

She pushed him away and stood up. "I'm glad you think this is funny."

Lafe came up behind her. He loved seeing her hair all wild with curls. "Look, we got a little carried away. The next time we'll have to keep our hands off each other at the site."

She swung around. "Next time! You think there's going to be a next time? I don't make a habit of sneaking around closets and letting men grope me."

Lafe couldn't help but grin. "You let me."

Michelle sucked in a breath. "My mistake." She started for the door, but Lafe pulled her back.

"Lady, I'm getting a little tired of your hot-and-cold act." His smile had long disappeared, and so had his patience. "I didn't force you into anything. I kissed you—you kissed me back. You weren't complaining either when we were rolling around on the floor."

Michelle was seething with anger and humiliation. How could she have let this happen? And how was she going to walk away with her pride intact? "Like I said, it was a mistake."

When Lafe started toward her, Michelle resisted the urge to back away. "Maybe you can lie to yourself," Lafe said, "but I don't believe a word of it. And I'm too old and too tired to play games. I want more out of life than my job." He glanced down at the spot on the carpet they had heated up only minutes ago. "And I thought for a few crazy moments that you might have wanted the same."

Michelle shut her eyes. "I told you, Lafe, that I can't."

"I know." He raised his hand. "All you want is a business relationship. Well, you've finally gotten through to me." He turned toward the door. "I won't be bothering you anymore." He walked out and left her there alone.

She pushed back the lump in her throat. She closed her eyes, her heart aching with pain. "Dammit, this is for the best," she whispered. "It's for the best."

Chapter Eight

Lafe braced his dusty boot against the porch railing and stared toward the San Juan Mountain Range. Rows of giant evergreen pines blanketed the peaks, reaching upward to the endless blue Colorado sky. He drew a deep breath of the cool air and tipped his straw Stetson back on his head. His thoughts went to Michelle, as they had every waking hour since he'd arrived at the ranch late Friday evening.

Two days and twelve hours of backbreaking work still couldn't drive her from his mind. Lafe's booted foot dropped to the new porch floor and he stood up. It wasn't supposed to be like this when he'd decided to take the Ocean Bluff job. He leaned against the post, remembering the sparks that had flown between him and Michelle when they had met in Colorado. He'd seen no reason that they couldn't pick up where they'd left off. With a casual relationship, nothing more. Just two consenting adults. Why not? It had been over a year since her husband's death.

But Lafe found that he didn't feel casual toward Michelle. What he did feel was protective, caring and excited about life for the first time in a long while. Just one of her smiles could turn him on faster than he would have ever imagined possible. He also felt frustrated and jealous, and he wanted to hit something every time he thought about the agony Tom Royer had put her through during their marriage. And T.J.? How could a father reject his son?

Of course, Lafe knew all about rejection. His own parents' desertion had been etched permanently in his memory. He knew how lonely it could be when no one cared about you. At least T.J. was lucky in that respect; he had his mother and the rest of her family.

Over the years, Lafe had never thought too much about settling down with a wife, a family. Starting a relationship had been difficult with his work and travel. Besides, it had been a long time since Lafe had allowed himself to get close to anyone. It was better that way.

He looked around the ranch, at all the improvements he'd made the past year. When he had taken over the big, two-story clapboard house, it was nearly falling down. Now, after remodeling the kitchen and replacing the roof and porch, not to mention slathering on gallons of paint inside and out, it was starting to look like a real home.

He glanced toward the two new barns that he had replaced six months ago, along with the large corral, now holding one of his mares and her two-week-old colt. In a few months, when he retired from the business, he would finally have all the time in the world to do what he wanted. He tugged his hat down to shade his eyes from the bright sun and headed toward the barn.

Why all of a sudden did it feel like a lonely proposition?

Michelle was at the site early Monday morning. "Where's Lafe?" she questioned Jeff.

"In Colorado."

"Is he bidding on a job?"

Jeff shook his head. "No, he's at his ranch. He'll be back today. Maybe I can help you."

Michelle couldn't believe that Lafe would just take off. Didn't he know that they had an open house scheduled in four days? Not to mention the fact they were still being ripped off.

"Over the weekend I was going over our inventory sheet and it's coming up short again."

"Darn, I was hoping that the stealing would stop after we hired extra security." He glanced over the paper Michelle handed him. "You want to come with me to the airport? You can tell Lafe about it yourself."

Michelle shook her head. She hadn't talked to Lafe since their time together in the closet and she was going to put it off as long as possible. "Just give him the list. I'll be here tomorrow." She turned and left the trailer.

Michelle berated herself all the way back to the office. She was running again and she had to stop. So she had made a mistake in allowing Lafe to kiss her. The biggest mistake was to dwell on it. Yet she couldn't help replaying in her head how it felt to be in the man's arms, how his lips had caressed her skin, how he'd managed to drive her control out the window. She felt her face flush. Dear Lord! she had nearly begged him to make love to her again, and in a closet for God's sake. All these weeks she'd been telling him to keep things on a business level, and the first chance she'd had she'd jumped into his arms and poured out her soul about her disastrous marriage. The worst part was she was falling for the man, and falling hard.

How in the world was she going to survive until Ocean Bluff was completed?

In her office Michelle worked most of the morning undisturbed, a little disappointed that she didn't get a phone call from Lafe, telling her that he was back. She sighed and dropped her pen on the desk as she stood up. *What's wrong with me?* she wondered. *Now I'm jealous because Lafe has a place to escape to for a few days.*

Michelle remembered Lafe's enthusiasm when he talked about his ranch. T.J. mentioned it all the time. Her son probably could tell her where it was, how big it was and the names of all the horses. To her shock, Michelle wanted to know more about the place, too. It seemed she knew nearly nothing about the Colorado cowboy.

That wasn't exactly true. Michelle's cheeks warmed. She did know that he would be a wonderful lover. She remembered how his hands and lips— Stop it! she cried silently.

The sudden knock on the door made Michelle spin around to find Betty peering inside.

"Got a few minutes?" Betty asked.

Michelle smiled. "Sure. I need a break."

"Boy, do you know how hard it is to get hold of you these days?" Betty plopped down in a chair.

"I've been busy." Michelle sat across from her friend. "I'm a little involved with this Ocean Bluff project."

"No kidding. Dad put me in charge of catering the open house this weekend. He told me to go all out." Betty smiled. "I've seen the completed model. It's gorgeous. You and Lafe should be proud of yourselves. You two make quite a team." She wiggled her eyebrows. "In more ways than one, I bet."

"And you're dreaming again."

"Too bad you're not." Betty shook her head. "Such a waste of a good man."

Michelle sighed. "C'mon, Betty. We are working together on a project. Besides, when Ocean Bluff is finished, Lafe's moving back to Colorado."

"Colorado is nice. I bet T.J. would like it there."

"Look…" Michelle raised her hand in warning. "I know where this is probably leading, so let's change the subject."

"How about we discuss the company picnic? Dad put me in charge of that, too."

Michelle relaxed in the chair. "Betty, you love every minute of it."

"This year I'm going with the western theme. It seemed to be such a big hit at your birthday party, and several of the girls in the office are eager to have a chance to dance with Lafe again." Betty gave Michelle a sideways glance. "So you'd better find something dynamite to wear if you want to compete. Of course, the man doesn't see anyone else when you're in the room. You could get away with wearing a potato sack." Betty sighed dramatically. "I wish I could get that kind of devotion from a man."

"Betty..." Michelle made a weak protest, but the tightening in her chest let her know that she cared about Lafe, more than she dared to admit. She didn't want other women getting his attention. Suddenly her job, T.J. and the hurt from her past couldn't stop her from focusing on the man she had come to want like no other.

Michelle looked at her friend. "What do you think I should wear to get his attention?"

That weekend Michelle played the perfect hostess. She greeted all the visitors graciously, as if they were being welcomed into her own home. That was how Ben Stafford wanted it. They were advertising the perfect home, and by God, that's what they presented to the prospective buyers. The model home's interior decor was perfectly done in shades of blue and wine. The downstairs furniture was eighteenth century Georgian Court, and upstairs the master suite was done in romantic Country French. Everyone raved about the elegant beauty of the home.

The Staffords, Ben and Mary, acted as hosts, while Betty made sure everyone sampled the food and champagne. Michelle stood close by and answered questions, but spent most of the time avoiding Lafe. He chose to stand off in the distance, but he also answered questions about the house's construction. Michelle did notice that women seemed to be drawn to him, and Lafe seemed to enjoy it, too, with his ready smile. She saw him escort several ladies around, supposedly showing off the model's special features, which included the master suite's huge walk-in closets. She hated to think she was jealous, but she was.

Michelle couldn't begin to estimate how many people walked through the model that weekend. But she was sure that she had shaken every one of their hands. Finally, about five o'clock Sunday, they were about to close things up.

Ben smiled. "It was a success." He hugged his wife, Mary, who was standing at his side. He then looked around the kitchen. "I can't thank you enough, Michelle." He took her in his arms. "I know this was a tough weekend for all of you." He then turned to Lafe and shook his hand. "Thank you, too, Lafe. I know you would rather have been at your ranch."

Lafe smiled. "Hey, I've got plenty of time for that. We have a few more houses to sell first," he joked.

"Well, besides the seven presales, it looks like there are definitely two more. I'll need to meet with you and Michelle this week. We're going to have some couple coming out to the site to pick out their parcels. What would be a good day for the both of you?"

Lafe shrugged and looked at Michelle. "It doesn't matter to me. Let me know the day and I'll be around."

Michelle nodded. "Anytime is okay with me, too."

"Good." Ben smiled. "Now, I want to take everyone out to dinner."

Michelle tried not to panic, but the last thing she wanted to do was sit across from Lafe and have him ignore her all night. "Oh, Ben, thank you, but I can't. I really need to get home to T.J."

"I think I'll have to take a rain check if you don't mind, Ben," Lafe added. "I'm a little tired. I'll lock up here. You and the family go on."

"Okay, but I plan to treat you both to dinner," Ben announced to Lafe and Michelle. The older man took hold of his wife's and daughter's hands. "C'mon, we're still going to celebrate."

After the Staffords left, Michelle and Lafe were by themselves, except for some of the catering crew still cleaning up. It was awkward, to say the least, Michelle thought, knowing she should leave and fast. "Well, I'd better get going." She got the nerve to look up at Lafe. It was a mistake. He captured her eyes with his—there was an invitation in the smoldering depths. Michelle felt her heart racing, and she glanced away, her courage from the other day gone. She started for the door and Lafe followed her.

"Don't go on my account," he called.

Her back stiffened, but she kept walking. Couldn't he leave well enough alone? "I'm not," she called back. "I need to get home." Which was a lie. T.J. was spending the night with a friend.

Michelle stopped and turned around. Lafe was standing in the entry with his hands on his hips. He was dressed in a pair of western-cut charcoal gray dress pants and black boots. His white western shirt was starched, and the sleeves were rolled up to expose his tanned forearms. No wonder she was attracted to him. He looked fantastic. But she couldn't think about him as a man right now; she had to think about him as the contractor for Ocean Bluff.

She held back a groan as he crossed his arms over his chest and his smoldering green eyes bored into hers. It was already too late.

Michelle stared at the numbers on her calculator, then looked at the figures on the inventory sheet. For the second time they didn't match.

"Damn!" She had been trying to find the shortages all Saturday morning. Slowly and subtly, materials had been disappearing on a regular basis. And Michelle was fed up with it. She knew it happened all the time on building sites, but that didn't make it right, particularly considering the replacement costs of specially ordered items such as brass hinges and doorknobs, fancy kitchen and bathroom fixtures, and Italian tile.

Michelle sat down on one of the wooden crates and glanced around the shed containing the building supplies, which was surrounded by a chain-link fence. It was locked tightly after working hours, and they had security. She knew Lafe and Jeff were still taking turns keeping guard many nights, hoping to catch the thieves in the act. Michelle wondered if she should stay one night, too.... Her thoughts turned to Lafe. She knew the last thing he wanted was to spend any more time with her than need be. The man had barely spoken to her in the past week, and only then when it pertained to business. And she missed their talks.

Lafe seemed to make things run smoother. Best of all, he never treated her any differently than he did the men. She knew he also had a lot to do with the crew's sudden change of attitude toward her.

But what would happen if their relationship turned personal? Darn, why couldn't they just be friends? She knew it was possible. She'd managed it with Jeff and Chris. Of course, she never felt as if she couldn't breathe when they were in the same room, and just making eye contact with them didn't cause her heart to race the way it did with Lafe Colter.

Michelle leaned back against a box and closed her eyes as a warm, familiar tingle ran down her spine. She remembered how Lafe's kisses had made her legs weak, and how the feel of his roughened hands on her skin made her come alive. She shifted restlessly. Just thinking about Lafe caused her nipples to grow taut. She sighed and imagined she heard someone call her. No, she had heard her name. Her eyes flew open to find Lafe standing in front of her.

"Lafe!" Embarrassed, she quickly sat up straight. "What are you doing here?"

"Looking for you," he replied. "We weren't able to reach you." He glanced around. "Where's the cellular phone?"

"I guess it's in the office." She stood. "Why, is something wrong?"

His eyes were filled with concern as he moved closer. "There's been an accident. They had to take T.J. to the hospital."

Her hands went to her mouth. She was terrified of what he was going to say. "Oh, my God! What happened?"

"Seems he took a spill off his bike and was knocked unconscious for a few minutes."

"I've got to go to him." Michelle started out of the shed, but Lafe grabbed her by the arm.

"I'll take you. You're in no condition to drive yourself."

"Okay, but please hurry." She didn't care who drove, she just wanted to get to her son.

No sooner had Lafe pulled the truck into the hospital parking lot than Michelle jumped out and headed for the emergency room doors. Lafe caught up with her as she reached the information desk.

"Where's my son?" she asked the nurse standing behind the counter.

The middle-aged woman gave both Lafe and Michelle a quick glance, then turned to the computer screen. "Patient's name?" she asked.

"T.J.—Thomas Joseph Royer," Michelle answered in a voice verging on hysteria. "He's seven years old. My father, Michael Donovan, came in with him about thirty minutes ago."

The nurse nodded. "Royer, Thomas J. is being examined by the doctor now." She looked at Michelle. "We'll have further information for you just as soon as the physician has finished."

"But... but I have to be with him. He's just a little boy."

"I know, and believe me, he's being well cared for."

The woman seemed apologetic, but Michelle felt as though she wanted to scratch her eyes out.

"I'll go check on his condition and get back to you." The nurse turned and walked through the double doors.

"Michelle?"

Both Lafe and Michelle turned to find Michael Donovan coming from the waiting area. Michelle rushed to her father. "Dad, what happened?"

Michael looked at Lafe. "Thanks for bringing her."

"Anytime." Lafe saw the strain on Michael's face. He didn't know the extent of T.J.'s injuries, but if the boy had been unconscious, he knew they had to be serious.

"From what Margaret said," Michael began, "he was playing with the boy next door."

"Jared Nelson?" Michelle gave a puzzled look. "He's twelve years old."

Michael raised a calming hand. "It seems Jared and his friends built a ramp in their backyard and were jumping it on their bikes. T.J. wanted to try, and they let him." Michael exchanged a glance with Lafe. "Well, he landed off balance, hitting his head."

"Oh, God!" Michelle sucked in a sharp breath and Lafe placed a protective arm around her shoulders.

"Don't worry, sport. He told me to tell you that he'll get back to see you later. That's if you behave yourself and don't give your mother and the doctors any trouble. He's even going to bring you a surprise."

"Wow!" T.J. smiled crookedly.

"What's all this noise in here?"

Everyone looked toward the door, to find a pleasant man in his early thirties, wearing a white lab coat.

"Hi, I'm Dr. David Johnson." He smiled readily. "I was on duty when they brought this guy in." He walked to the bed and shook hands with Michelle and her father.

"Doctor, how bad are my son's injuries?" Michelle asked.

The young doctor took a moment to look over the chart. "Well, T.J. has a slight concussion, a gash on his forehead and some laceration of the face and chin. He's bruised a couple of ribs and he'll be sore all over for a few days. As a precaution, I'd like to keep him here overnight for observation.

"What do you think, T.J?" he asked, directing his attention to the child in the bed. "Can you put up with hospital food until tomorrow at noon?"

For the first time since the ordeal had started, T.J. looked frightened. "Can...can my mom stay, too?"

The doctor glanced at Michelle. "She can stay if she wants to. But we're taking you upstairs to the children's ward. You're probably going to have a roommate, so if you're worried about getting lonely..."

T.J.'s eyes lit up. "Maybe she can stay a little while," he agreed.

Michelle realized that everything seemed to be an adventure to her child. How was she going to survive until he was grown?

While T.J. was being taken to the third floor, Michelle went to the admitting desk and gave them her insurance card. Within thirty minutes she was sitting at T.J.'s bedside. Michael Donovan arrived with books and magazines from the hospital gift shop, giving Michelle a chance to borrow her father's car and run home for a quick shower.

By seven o'clock she was back at the hospital, talking her father into going home. T.J. had eaten some dinner, but was restless. She could tell that his injuries were bothering him. She sat on the edge of the bed and gently stroked his arms. That seemed to help and he closed his eyes. She knew his sleep would be interrupted when the nurses came in to check on him, but he could rest for now, anyway. She brushed the curls off T.J.'s forehead with a shaky hand, thanking God for watching over her child today. She knew his injuries could have been much worse. And what if she couldn't have been reached? Her tears fell and she quickly wiped them off her cheeks.

A large figure cast a shadow across the bed. She turned and found Lafe. He was holding a metal balloon tied to a red ribbon in one hand and a paper sack in the other. He must have gone home and changed into his usual jeans and boots. He gave her a smile and came closer. "I won't stay long. I just wanted to check and see if the kid's okay." Lafe stopped next to the bed railing and looked down at T.J.

Michelle could see by the expression on his face that he was worried, though he was attempting not to let on.

"He sure tried hard to beat himself up, didn't he?" Lafe glanced at Michelle, then back to the child asleep in the bed. "Are you sure he's going to be okay?"

Michelle nodded. "The doctor said there will be a lot of bruises and soreness and he has a slight concussion."

Lafe held out the white paper sack. "Here. Thought you could use some food." He went to the end of the bed and looped the balloon string to the railing, while Michelle looked inside the bag and found a couple of hamburgers and some fries.

"Thanks, I guess I forgot to eat." She popped a fry into her mouth. "You want some, too?"

"No, I brought the other one for T.J. But I guess he's out for the night."

"He'll probably wake up soon. Those bruised ribs are causing him some discomfort."

Lafe could only stare at the sleeping boy. T.J. looked so damn helpless, and there wasn't a thing he could do to take the pain away. All at once the child made a whimpering sound and began to move. Lafe took hold of his hand. "Whoa, partner, take it easy."

T.J. blinked open his eyes and tried to smile. "Lafe...you came." He was fighting hard to stay awake. "Don't go, please...."

Lafe sat down on the bed. "How about I hang around until you fall asleep? Then I'll come and visit you at home in a few days. When you can stay awake."

"Okay...." T.J.'s eyelids drooped and finally closed.

Michelle watched as Lafe just stared at her son. The pain she saw in the man's eyes was real. Somewhere in his past he had been hurt...deeply. And it made her hurt, too. She found that she wanted to reach out and comfort him in the same way he had comforted her earlier. But she knew that things wouldn't stop with just comfort. And she couldn't give him any more. She just couldn't.

Michelle released a tired sigh. She already had too much to cope with and didn't need this man complicating her life any more than he already had. "I think he'll be out for a while. So...so if you have to leave, it's okay."

Lafe's expression grew hard and resentful. "Don't worry, Michelle, I'm not getting any ideas about pushing my way into your life. I'm just concerned about the boy." He got up from the bed, his eyes riveted on her. "I'm not like your husband was, so don't make me pay for his sins." He started across the room and stopped. "When T.J. wakes up, tell him I'll be in touch."

As Lafe disappeared into the hall, Michelle sat at her son's bedside. Unintentionally she had hurt Lafe. Tears formed in her eyes. She wanted to call him back. But in the long run, maybe it was for the best that he had gone. Best for her survival.

The nurse came in to check on T.J. "Your husband sure is a nice man. And so concerned about your boy. We don't let visitors in after-hours, but we make exceptions for family."

Michelle stared at the woman. *Lafe had told her that he was T.J.'s father?*

"And of course," the woman continued, "after your husband explained that he had been out of town on business and rushed home to see his son . . . Well, I think you're both pretty lucky to have a man like that in your life."

Michelle felt more tears forming in her eyes. "Yes, we are pretty lucky."

Chapter Nine

Two weeks had passed since T.J.'s accident, and he was
almost fully recovered. Except for a faint scar over his eye,
no one would ever know anything had happened. Michelle
found that keeping her child down the past fourteen days
had been the roughest part. A new video game from Uncle
Joe and numerous coloring books and puzzles from
Grandpa and Margaret had helped entertain the restless patient.

Lafe had done the most good, frequently dropping by
after work to visit with T.J. They'd spend an hour or so
telling stories or talking about what T.J. referred to as
"ranch stuff." It didn't take long for Michelle to realize that
the two were becoming good friends.

She'd often heard laughter, and felt a little left out that
she was never invited to join in the fun. She'd even cooked
her son's favorite meals and given him more ice cream than
she should have, but hadn't received near the praise that
Lafe had when he'd presented T.J. with an old rope. Ac-
cording to T.J. the rope was special. It was one that Lafe
had used in the rodeo. How could she compete with a trea-
sure like that?

Finally Dr. Johnson pronounced T.J. fit to return to normal activity. The first thing on the schedule was the Stafford Investments Company picnic. T.J. had been waiting all summer for this and Michelle knew there was no way she could talk him out of going. And she would have a lot of explaining to do herself if she didn't show up.

The day of the picnic Michelle turned her car into the large circular drive of the Stafford home in Orange Acres. She parked her VW in the last vacant spot. The party was in full swing, judging by the number of cars crowded in the driveway. She noticed one in particular, a truck parked by the birch tree. Lafe was already here.

T.J. took off as Michelle pulled in a deep breath to calm herself before stepping out of her car. Her gaze took in the well-kept lawn and manicured shrubs lining the property. She smiled as she looked at the familiar two-story flagstone house. Hunter green shutters framed every window, shining brightly as if they were freshly painted.

"C'mon, Mom," T.J. called, already standing on the porch. "Everybody's here."

She grabbed her things and hurried after him. "Okay, but no running. You still have to take it easy."

"I can go swimming. Dr. Dave said."

Michelle rang the bell. "But you can't overdo it."

"Oh, Mom...."

Betty answered the door and greeted them. T.J. said hello and headed toward the pool.

"I gather he's feeling better," Betty commented.

"I still want him to take it easy."

"Don't worry, there are plenty of adults around to keep a lookout on the kids," Betty assured her, eyeing the plastic bag. "What's in the garment bag?"

"Just what I'm wearing tonight," Michelle said nonchalantly.

"Really, let me see."

Michelle pulled the bag out of her friend's reach. "I'll show you only if you let me change in your old bedroom."

"Well, what are we waiting for?" Betty tugged on Michelle's arm as she walked up the spiral staircase. "Did you bring a swimsuit, too?"

"Yeah, but—"

"No buts," Betty argued, then stopped on the stairs. "Remember, there are a lot of women out there with plans to snag a cowboy."

Michelle rolled her eyes. Why had she ever confided in Betty? All she'd told her friend was that if she ever thought about getting serious about another man, she might consider someone like Lafe. Now, of course, she had to accept the fact that she might have blown her chance. Lately the man acted as if he wanted nothing to do with her.

"Betty, there's no way I can begin to look like those twenty-one-year-old secretaries from the office," she said defeatedly as they walked into the cluttered bedroom that still showed traces of a teenager's room. "They all have legs up to their eyebrows, and unless you've discovered a way to stretch me..."

"Hey! You've got enough curves on that five-foot-three-inch body to keep a man interested." Betty gave Michelle a convincing glance. "You just haven't learned to show them off...yet."

"Oh, brother! Why do I have this feeling you're going to give me a crash course?"

"Stop worrying. I'll take care of it," Betty assured her as she hung Michelle's garment bag on a hook in the closet. "I'm just tickled you decided to come back to the living. I know you went through a lot during your marriage, but it's time to put it in the past. And a man like Lafe Colter is just what you need."

"But, Betty, what if he's decided that he doesn't want me anymore?"

Her friend patted her hand. "Don't worry. After what I have planned, the man won't have a chance."

Michelle's heart sank. Betty always had more guts than she did. Went after what she wanted, and usually got it. Michelle wasn't like that. Maybe that was the reason Tom had found her so easy to control all those years. She drew a long, strengthening breath. She wanted to change. And she wanted Lafe Colter.

Thirty minutes later, Michelle timidly followed Betty to the pool. She'd put on a two-piece suit, but it didn't seem to cover as much as it had when she'd tried it on in the dressing room at the store. At least Betty had loaned her a short terry robe.

After checking on T.J., Betty and Michelle sat down next to the pool. "Do you see him yet?"

"Who?" Michelle asked.

Betty turned to her friend. "Lafe, of course. Who else would I be looking for?"

"Well, since you're married, I thought you just might be trying to find your husband." Michelle didn't want her friend playing matchmaker. "By the way, where is Bill?"

"Oh, he's around somewhere." Betty shrugged. "I'm needed here with you."

Michelle was running short on patience. "Betty, you don't have to stay with me. You're supposed to play hostess for your parents' party. I'm just going to sit here and try to relax." Michelle pulled her hair into a ponytail and twisted a rubber band around it, then leaned back and exposed her face to the sun. "If Lafe wants to be with me—which I doubt—he can find me."

"Great attitude!" her friend cheered her.

"Betty!" A familiar voice called from the shallow end of the pool. It was Betty's husband, Bill.

"Hi, Bill." Michelle waved, and he waved back.

Bill Thomas was an attractive man. He stood well over six feet, and his sandy-colored hair was streaked with a little gray around the temples. His build wasn't bad, but it couldn't compare with Lafe's. Darn! Michelle shook her head, as if to drive the man from her thoughts. "Betty, go to your husband."

"Only if you promise me one thing," she said, kicking off her sandals.

Michelle released a tired breath. "I know I'm going to regret this, but what?"

"Take off the robe and at least get some sun. You look like you're going to pass out from the heat." Betty strolled off to the shallow end of the pool as her husband and son, Billy greeted her.

Anything to keep her friend off her back, Michelle thought. Stripping away the robe, she laid it on the back of her chair, but before she got a chance to enjoy the sun she heard a whistle.

"Wow! Michelle, is that you?" asked someone from behind her.

Michelle turned toward Chris Lawson. "Oh, Chris, you startled me." She tried to hide her embarrassment over his exaggerated stare.

"Boy, oh, boy, you look...great." He shook his head. "Here!" He offered her one of the two drinks he held. "You look like you could use this."

"Thank you for the compliment—and the drink." She took the wine cooler and sipped it as Chris sat down.

"I'm glad to see you made the party. You've been putting in some long hours at Ocean Bluff, plus taking care of your son. I kind of miss not seeing you around the office."

"Oh, Chris, that's sweet." She smiled. "But don't worry, I'll be back before you know it. Another six weeks and the project should be completed."

"How are you holding up with Colter?"

"Not bad." Michelle was a little nervous as she wondered if there had been any office gossip floating around about her and Lafe. "I've had some trouble with a few of the men, but Lafe has treated me fairly."

Chris accepted her answer and was filling her in on his last project, when she heard T.J. calling her.

She spotted her son at the edge of the pool, his elbows resting against the concrete side. "Hi, T.J.," she called back.

"C'mere, Mom. I have something to tell you."

Michelle went to the side of the pool and knelt. Her son giggled when suddenly he popped out of the pool, riding on a pair of broad shoulders. Lafe's.

"Gotcha, Mom." T.J. giggled again, then jumped into the water.

"I'm glad you think it's so funny scaring your mother. And besides, you're supposed to take it easy," she chided her son, but her gaze was on Lafe as he came toward her. He was standing in only five feet of water, so his glorious upper body was in plain view. Her heart rate began to accelerate.

"Hello, Michelle," Lafe greeted her, while his gaze wandered over her body. "Lord, woman! Are you tryin' to do in half the males here with that suit?" he whispered in a husky voice.

Although Michelle had seen Lafe at work, and at her house when he'd visited T.J., this was the first time he had actually spoken to her other than to be polite or for business. She smiled. "No, just trying to get someone's attention." *His*.

"I think you have." Lafe's hand shot out of the water, grabbing her by the wrist and pulling her into the pool.

"Oh!" she gasped at the shock of cold water.

Lafe held her by the arms as she treaded water. "Thought you might be getting a little too hot." He glanced to where Michelle had been sitting next to Chris Lawson.

She looked back at Chris and returned his wave. It dawned on her. Could Lafe be jealous?

"C'mon, Mom. Swim with us," T.J coaxed, splashing water in her face.

Michelle turned away to avoid the spray, but it was too late. Wiping the water from her face, she hurried to catch up with her son to pay him back, but before she could reach him he had climbed out of the pool—thanks to Lafe, who had grabbed her by the ankle, slowing her down. She turned in an effort to splash Lafe, but he laughed and swam away. His long smooth strokes made her feel clumsy just trying to keep up.

The water felt so refreshing, and with some encouragement from Lafe and T.J., Michelle decided to stay in for a while. They swam and raced, and her son even showed off a few of his dives. T.J. eventually met up with Billy and they swam off together, leaving Michelle alone with Lafe.

They continued to swim lazily in the tepid water, until fatigue and other swimmers drove Michelle to the side of the pool. Lafe followed close behind.

"Boy, I'm out of shape," she gasped.

"I wouldn't say that." Lafe's gaze went to her bikini top. "You seem to be able to keep up."

"Just barely," she admitted as his hand went to her waist, directing her away from the kids who were splashing. The next thing she knew both his arms were on either side of her, trapping her between him and the concrete wall. Nervously looking around the pool, Michelle hoped to spot T.J. and find an excuse to break his hold. Not that Lafe was actually holding her, or even touching her . . . but he was close. Too close.

Lafe knew he was acting crazy. Michelle had let him know more than once that she wanted nothing to do with him outside of business. Now here they were, behaving like a couple of teenagers. But Lafe wasn't playing. He wanted Michelle, and she wanted him. She just didn't know it yet.

"T.J. sure is having fun," he said, trying to keep the conversation going. Otherwise he might devour her and her cute little bikini right there in the pool.

"Maybe too much."

"How about you?" His leg brushed against hers accidentally. "Are you having a good time?"

"Yes, I'm having a wonderful time," she answered. Just then a swimmer went by and splashed them both. Lafe wiped water from his face and Michelle shivered.

"Cold?" he asked.

"No," Michelle answered truthfully. If anything, she was hot and getting hotter as she was being drawn to Lafe's mesmerizing green eyes. And she seemed on the verge of melting, when a too-coy woman's voice rang out, causing them to turn around.

"Lafe—oh, Lafe."

"It's Carrie," Lafe said.

Michelle located Betty's younger sister standing beside the pool with her hands on her hips—and that was about the only thing that covered that area of her body. Carrie Stafford was the perfect California girl: light-blond, shoulder-length hair, blue eyes, a deeply tanned, shapely body, long legs.... The twenty-three-year-old woman wasn't stupid, either. She had graduated from UCLA the previous spring with a degree in business. And from what Betty had told Michelle, she was husband hunting.

Carrie flashed Lafe a bright smile. "I've been looking for you everywhere. C'mon, you promised to help me with the children's races."

"Sorry, I guess I forgot the time."

Finally Carrie seemed to notice there was someone else in the pool. "Oh, Michelle, hi."

"Hi, Carrie," Michelle said through clenched teeth.

The young woman turned her attention back to Lafe. "I'll go change and meet you in ten minutes."

"Okay," Lafe agreed as he pulled himself up onto the edge of the pool. He sat there a moment, watching as Carrie walked to the house, then he looked down at Michelle. "Sorry, duty calls. Thanks for the swim." He stood and walked away.

"Anytime," Michelle replied. She wasn't going to give him the satisfaction of knowing that she was bothered by his leaving her for another woman. After all, didn't she want Lafe to direct his attention to someone else? Michelle climbed out of the pool and pulled on her robe. Lafe needed someone who wasn't trying to rebuild her life and make a career for herself. Someone who wanted to give her heart freely, without being afraid to lose herself.

After Michelle changed back into her shorts and top, she returned to the pool area to find her son. Instead she met Ben and Mary. They chatted about old times and discussed Ocean Bluff, before Michelle excused herself to look for her missing child.

The Stafford home sat on two acres of land. The back-yard was beautifully landscaped with rolling green turf and several large shade trees, where a group of kids were gathered.

"Hey, Mom," T.J. yelled as he ran across the grass toward her. "Look—we won a blue ribbon." His eyes were large, and he was holding up a box of candy.

"Who's 'we'—you and Billy?"

"No." The boy shook his head. "Me and Lafe. We won the three-legged race. Boy, Mom, he's really good, and we were so fast that none of the other fathers and sons could catch us. Wait until I show Grandpa and Uncle Joe." T.J. grinned happily and pinned the ribbon to his shirt.

"That's great. And that was awful nice of Lafe to race with you." Michelle looked around for Lafe, to thank him, but her smile disappeared when she saw Carrie hanging on his arm.

"Mom, I'm going back now. They're having more races."

"Okay, son. But be careful." She watched T.J. run off, then turned her attention to Lafe and the tall blonde next to him. They seemed engrossed in each other, and every so often Carrie would rest her hand on Lafe's arm. Michelle tensed, her fists clenched. She wanted to shout out to Carrie to keep her hands off Michelle's man. But that was insane! One baseball game and a few kisses didn't make Lafe Colter hers.

Betty suddenly appeared. "Doesn't it just make you sick? And here I thought my sister went for the Wall Street type. She's probably just playing around."

Michelle tried to look unconcerned. "He doesn't seem to mind."

"Just wait until he sees you at the barbecue tonight. He'll forget all about Carrie," Betty said assuredly.

The afternoon wore on, and the races and games finally ended. T.J. won another blue ribbon and two red ones. Now over a dozen kids were hungry and were waiting at the picnic tables for their food—hamburgers and hot dogs. Ben stood at the head of the line, announcing the activities after dinner. A movie was planned to entertain the kids while the adults ate and danced.

After Michelle got T.J. settled in the family room, she retreated upstairs to change for dinner. Betty had dressed earlier, so Michelle had the room to herself. She was in and out of the shower in ten minutes, then quickly applied her makeup and dried her hair. It was still a little damp when she pulled it up on top of her head, brushed a few wispy bangs across her forehead and arranged some loose curls around her ears and her nape. Pleased with the result, she walked back to the adjoining bedroom to dress.

The Stafford patio had been transformed for the night's activities. Long buffet tables were crowded with food as the caterers worked. Several smaller tables covered with red checkered cloths circled the lit pool. Most everyone had already changed into evening dress and had gathered on the patio, sharing drinks and conversation.

Lafe had on a pair of black jeans and a brightly-colored western shirt. Glancing down at his shiny black boots, he grinned. *They wanted a cowboy—they'll get a cowboy.* Maybe he should go to his truck for his Stetson. That would complete the image.

Instead he searched the patio area for the dozenth time. Where was Michelle? He hadn't seen her come out of the house yet. He had wanted to spend more time with her today, but had ended up with Carrie and, of course, T.J. He'd never thought he would have such a good time with the boy. He took another drink from his glass of ginger ale and looked back toward the French doors. A hunger that had nothing to do with food gnawed at his gut as Michelle walked onto the patio.

"Beautiful..." he breathed into the warm July night air.

The off-the-shoulder white blouse she wore caught the curve of her full breasts and showed off her recent tan. Her blue print gathered skirt swayed against her shapely legs as she strolled around the patio. She stopped to talk to friends, but quickly moved on again as if she were looking for someone. Silently Lafe hoped it was him. Then finally, almost if he'd willed it, their eyes met. He smiled first, then watched patiently as she returned the smile. Shyly, her hands clasped in front of her, she walked toward him. His spirits soared when he saw that the delicate shamrock charm he had gotten her for her birthday was draped around her slender neck.

Just keep it light or you'll blow it, he told himself as they met in the middle of the patio.

"You look lovely," he murmured.

She seemed surprised by the compliment. Her cheeks flushed and she lowered her eyes. "Thank you."

"Can I get you something to drink?"

"No... no, thank you." She looked away hastily. "I'll wait until dinner." Then after a moment her gaze drifted back to meet his. "Lafe," she whispered. "I'd like to thank you for running with T.J. in the three-legged race. It's all he talked about all afternoon."

"My pleasure. I enjoyed it, too."

"It was nice of you to take the time. And about your coming over to the house last week... You really helped with his recovery. I realize it took a lot of your free time."

"You'd have your hands full trying to keep him down." He leaned closer. "Besides, I like T.J. He's a good kid."

Lafe was surprised when she didn't pull back. Instead her gaze sought his.

"It was still kind of you. Jeff said you postponed a trip to your ranch."

He shrugged. "I'll be living there before too long."

In a comfortable silence, their eyes locked, while the outside world moved around them. Lafe was only aware of Michelle.

"Oh, Lafe, there you are."

Both turned, to see Carrie crossing the patio toward them. Lafe glanced at Michelle, disappointed their moment was lost. With a tense smile, he greeted Carrie.

Michelle felt the hair on the back of her neck stand up as the blonde approached. She was dressed in tight jeans tucked into a pair of beautifully tooled western boots. Her rust-colored silk blouse highlighted her hair—not to mention her small firm breasts.

"I bet you two were talking business," Carrie scolded, raising her hand. "Now, don't deny it. This is a party. You can talk about Ocean Bluff on Monday. Anyway, the steaks are ready." Carrie flashed her baby blues. "C'mon, I'm hungry, cowboy."

Chris Lawson appeared at Michelle's side. "Sorry, I'm late," he apologized. "I guess I got sidetracked. You ready to eat?"

Michelle stared at Chris. Where did he come from? Then she saw how he was eyeing Carrie Stafford with interest.

Lafe spoke next. "Why don't we all sit together?"

Michelle knew she wasn't about to spend the evening watching the two of them together. "I'm sorry," she said. "I promised Betty that I'd eat with her and Bill."

After a trip through the food line, Michelle went looking for Betty, hoping that Lafe and Carrie would decide to sit elsewhere. She found her friend at a table at the far side of the pool.

"Michelle, you look terrific," Betty said, eyeing her outfit.

"Thanks." Michelle sat her plate of food on the table, then dropped into the chair next to her friend. "Betty, what am I doing here?" Michelle found herself dangerously close to tears. "This was a crazy idea. I'm going home to try to forget this day." She started to get up.

"You'll do no such thing." Betty grabbed her arm and made her sit down again. "How many times do I have to tell you it's obvious that Lafe cares about you? You're not going to give up. I saw how the man practically drooled when you came out to the patio." She got a mischievous glint in her eyes. "Maybe you should go after him?"

Michelle held back a groan, remembering that time in Colorado. How her first and only attempt had ended in disaster. She released a long sigh. "Look, I'm no good at this."

"Then just leave everything to me," her friend instructed. "I've got a plan."

"Oh, Lord, no, Betty. I'll stay for a while, but...if you do anything to embarrass..." Michelle shook her finger.

Lafe and Carrie and a very attentive Chris had found their way to the table and joined them. Chris did everything for Michelle except cut her meat, but she had the feeling that if she asked he wouldn't hesitate to oblige her. She kept sending him questioning looks, but he ignored them.

Surprisingly the conversation over dinner was pleasant; even Carrie seemed easy to talk to. In fact, Carrie spent quite a bit of time talking with Chris. And every time Michelle glanced in Lafe's direction she found that he was watching her. Then he'd smile and she'd feel her cheeks flush.

In keeping with the party's theme, they had hired a country-and-western band. When they began to play the first song, several couples hurried to the dancing area on the large patio. Betty went off with Bill, Carrie pulled Lafe onto the floor and Chris insisted Michelle also dance.

As they moved in time with the music, Michelle looked up at Chris. "Okay," she began. "What are you and Betty up to?"

Chris gave her a puzzled look. "What are you talking about?" he asked, trying not to smile.

"Deny it if you want, Mr. Lawson, but I know something is going on." Michelle grinned. "It's just a good thing you're so important to Stafford Investments, because you'd starve as an actor."

"Let's just hope it works out for the both of us," Chris told her as he danced her around the floor. Finally the song ended to applause. Michelle thanked Chris and had started to return to her table, when she felt a slight tug on her arm. It was Lafe.

He smiled. "I believe this is our dance."

Michelle could only nod, then she glanced over her shoulder to see Chris take Carrie in his arms as the music began.

Suddenly excited, she quickly fell into step as Lafe glided her around the floor to the two-step beat. His eyes never left her face as they moved in tempo. With a smile Lafe began to spin her around several times, causing her skirt to swirl high above her knees. But Michelle's only concern was returning to Lafe's arms, and she did so without missing a step. By the time the song ended and the crowd began to applaud, they were both breathless and laughing. Michelle blushed as she tried to leave.

"Whoa...you can't go now." Lafe gripped her by the arm as the band leader announced the next song. "Ladies and gents, I hope you folks enjoy a nice slow one, because we have a dandy. We have a request to play it for a very special lady. 'Feels So Right,'" he breathed into the microphone.

Michelle went willingly into Lafe's arms. He immediately cradled her against his chest, resting his jaw along her temple as they swayed to the ballad. Shutting her eyes, Michelle felt only the rapid beating of her heart and the vibrations from his rich voice as he began to hum.

Michelle's body trembled with desire as she listened to the words of the song. The truth suddenly hit her. She wanted to be in Lafe's arms—she needed to be there. It felt so good, so right, wrapped in his protective embrace, shielded from the loneliness she thought she'd learned to accept.

She closed her eyes. Maybe needing a man in her life didn't have to make her weak, or even take away from her independence. Over the past few months, she had spent so much time running from the truth, she'd never stopped to see how much she had come to care for Lafe. Burying a gasp in Lafe's shirtfront, she succumbed to reality. She had fallen in love.

Lafe pulled her closer, causing her breasts to be pinned against his chest. Her legs turned to jelly when his thighs brushed hers lightly.

"I love holding you like this," he whispered in her ear.

"I...I like it, too," she managed to answer.

All too soon the music ended, and reluctantly they moved apart, but only by inches. "Thanks for the dance." Lafe's voice was husky; his eyes held hers.

She managed a smile. "Thank you."

"God—you're beautiful." He raised his hand to her face and stroked her cheek.

Michelle's eyes fluttered closed; her lips parted with longing just as Carrie's voice broke their intimate spell.

The blonde tugged on Lafe's arm. "Lafe, you promised me the next dance."

Suddenly feeling exposed, Michelle was glad of the semi-darkness that hid her embarrassment and the pain in her heart. "Excuse me," she said and made her exit.

Pushing her way across the crowded dance floor, Michelle quickly left the patio. She had to get away from Lafe—get away so he couldn't see how she truly felt.

After admitting to herself that she was in love with him, she was terrified. She hurried across the lawn, not caring that people were watching. Michelle knew she couldn't stand there and watch Lafe hold another woman in his arms.

She stopped at the back of the lawn, leaned against a big tree and pulled off her sandals. Had she made a fool of herself? Over and over she'd kept telling him that all she wanted was a business relationship. And then, out there on the dance floor, in front of all those people...

"Darn you, Lafe Colter! What are you trying to do to me?"

"Can't be any worse than what you have put me through."

Michelle gasped and turned, to see Lafe standing in the moonlight. "You...you startled me."

"Well, if you hadn't run off, I wouldn't have had to go searching for you." He stepped closer. "When are you going to stop running away from me?"

"I'm not running." *Oh, why can't I be honest?* she berated herself silently.

"I don't believe you." His expression softened as he pointed back toward the patio, where the soft sound of the band drifted in the night air. "Was that all an act? I don't think so. Why do you keep denying you have feelings for me?"

"I... I'm afraid," she confessed curtly.

"Lady, you've scared the hell out of me since the moment we met," he said right back. "That night you came into my room, it took everything I had to send you away. I wanted you so badly... I thought I'd go out of my mind."

Lafe watched the confused expression on Michelle's face. He had to jam his hands into his pockets to keep from reaching for her. Yet he knew instinctively that he had to give her some space.

"Then why did you send me away?"

"Michelle, you were hurting. I didn't want to be just any man to fill that physical need."

"But it was more than that—" She stopped and glanced away.

Lafe knew she'd revealed more than she had planned. "It was more for me, too." God, he was pouring out his heart, and she wasn't even facing him. "Look at me, Michelle."

She turned, wiping the tears off her cheeks, and Lafe hated himself for the pain he was causing her, but he also felt it was the time for Michelle to face some of her demons from the past and move on.

"What about now?" he asked. "Do you have feelings for me now?"

"Please, go back to Carrie."

Had he pushed her too far? "I don't want Carrie," he almost shouted, then softly said, "Dammit, woman! I've never wanted anyone as much as I want you."

The glowing Malibu lights circling the yard helped Lafe read the glint of surprise in Michelle's eyes.

"You want me . . . ?"

Lafe forgot to breathe, but managed to nod.

"Oh, Lafe. . . ." She threw her arms around his neck, holding him tight.

Smiling, Lafe lowered his head. "It's about time, lady. It's about time." Then his mouth took hers in a fierce kiss.

Chapter Ten

Michelle had watched Lafe gently place T.J. on his bed. The little guy had fallen asleep in the car on the way home, exhausted from all the day's activities. Lafe had followed her home in his truck and carried him into his room. Together they'd stripped him out of his clothes and tucked him in for the night.

Now Lafe turned to face her, and taking her hand, he walked back down the hall with her.

It was nearly midnight when they sat down on the overstuffed sofa in the dimly-lit living room. *Nervous* didn't begin to describe how Michelle was feeling at this moment. So many times in the past few weeks Lafe had visited her home, but this time it was different. Now, after he had said goodnight to T.J., he wasn't walking out the door—this time he was staying.

"Sorry you had to carry T.J. to bed," Michelle said apologetically. "I guess he was done in from the picnic."

Lafe grinned, pulling her into his arms. "At least he won't be getting up again." His mouth caressed the spot below her ear.

"Oh..." she gasped as he trailed kisses along her jaw to the sensitive area of her neck. "What...what did it cost you?"

"I just told him that if he went to sleep right away, you would bring him down to the beach house tomorrow and spend the day."

Michelle's heart soared higher. "All day?"

He pulled back and grinned at her again. "I'd prefer all day *and* all night. But I think I'd be pushing my luck, huh?"

Michelle's body felt hot and cold at the same time. *Oh, yes, I would love a whole night with you,* she wanted to scream, but luckily the words were stuck in her throat. She wasn't thinking rationally; she never did when she was near Lafe.

When his lips took hers, she melted into his arms. How had she ever lived without this for so long? she cried silently, returning his kiss with her own hungry one.

"Oh, Michelle...." He trailed his fingers along her neck to the edge of her blouse. He tugged its elastic top off her shoulders, tasting the newly exposed skin. Michelle's finger dug into his arms as he moved his hand to cover her breast. It didn't take long before the rosy nipple grew hard against his palm. "I want you...."

When his lips returned to hers, Michelle went crazy, her body responding with an eagerness she had never felt before. She felt as though she were drowning in her feelings. How could she ever have thought she truly loved Tom?

"I want you, too," she breathed, becoming the aggressor. Her arms moved around his neck, her mouth sought his; she didn't want this wonderful feeling ever to end.

Lafe raised his lips from Michelle's, only to return to her breasts, sending shivers of desire racing through her. She arched her back, trying to get closer.

Lafe leaned back on the sofa, pulling Michelle on top of him. She quickly tugged at his shirt. When the snaps gave way, she reached inside and began to stroke his chest.

A violent shudder shook him, and Lafe tore his mouth away. "Michelle...you're killing me." His breathing was harsh as he changed their position. Now he was on top, and her body was cradling his. As quick as she drew her next breath, Michelle shifted her legs, pulling herself flush against his hardness. Lafe grasped the back of her head, and he took her mouth in another wild, searing kiss.

Michelle was ready to surrender to her overwhelming need, when she heard T.J. calling out her name. With her last ounce of willpower, she managed to push Lafe away.

"Michelle?"

"T.J. wants me," she said. And as if on signal, the child cried out again. "Give me a minute." She needed more time than that to compose herself, but she didn't have the luxury. She adjusted her blouse and hurried off to her son's bedroom.

She found T.J. sitting up in bed, holding his stomach.

"What is it, honey?" She sat down beside him on the bed.

"I don't feel good, Mom. My tummy hurts."

"Could it be the three hot dogs, the pizza and the ice cream you had at the party?" she asked, knowing her son wasn't usually a complainer.

T.J. groaned. "Maybe."

"Be right back." She went into the bathroom and got the Pepto-Bismol. After she gave T.J. a good dose, he lay back down.

"How's he doing?" Lafe asked.

Michelle turned and almost collided with him as he leaned over her shoulder. "Just a little upset stomach."

The boy opened his eyes. "Lafe?" He tried to sit up.

"Whoa, there." Lafe reached out to stop the child's movement. "You've had a full day, partner. It's time for some shut-eye. I want you well rested so your mother and you can come to the beach house tomorrow."

"Can we go, Mom?"

Michelle nodded. "But only if you get some sleep." She pulled the covers around his shoulders, then leaned down and kissed his forehead.

"'Night, T.J." She got off the bed, and was surprised when Lafe reached down and hugged her son. Her chest suddenly tightened at the touching scene.

Lafe made sure that the boy was asleep, then he turned and followed Michelle out of the room and down the hall into the living room.

"Seems we're always getting interrupted." Lafe drew her into his arms, but he knew immediately she was no longer in a responsive mood.

"Maybe someone's trying to tell us something," she said, distancing herself from him.

What was she trying to tell him? Lafe ran his fingers through his hair in frustration and walked to the sofa. He sank down with a sigh, trying to ease the ache in his tense body.

Finally Michelle looked at him. "I think we need to talk, Lafe."

She ran her tongue over her still-swollen lips. Her cheeks showed a rosy blush; even her messy hair looked sexy. He watched as she nervously pulled the pins from her hair, allowing her dark mane to fall to her shoulders. The shoulders his lips had caressed a short time before—

He shook away the thought. "Then talk," he suggested.

Her dark gaze darted around the room, avoiding any contact with his. "Maybe this wasn't such a good idea...."

Lafe's heart began to pound wildly. No, he refused to let her run away again. It had taken him too long to get her to admit she cared for him. "You aren't telling me that you want to go back to a business relationship?"

Bravely Michelle turned to Lafe. Panic caused her stomach to knot with anxiety. She must not lose control, and the way she felt about Lafe, she knew that it would be impossible not to. "No, we can't do that now. It's just that...that we were moving too fast." She drew a long breath and blurted out, "I just can't go to bed with you."

"If you're saying you don't want me..." He pointed to the sofa, and she flushed, remembering all too well what had almost happened.

She hurried to stop him. "No! I'm just saying...that I'm not ready. It may be a long time...." She paused. "And I want you to know that if you change your mind—"

Lafe wasn't about to let her finish. He pulled her into his arms, crushing his mouth against hers. She made a purring sound and her lips parted to accept his stroking tongue. Finally he drew back, his breathing ragged as his body moved urgently, letting her know how much he wanted her. "Does that answer your question?"

Her eyes were bright with pleasure as she managed a nod.

"And I'm not planning on changing my mind." His hand cupped her face, his gaze searching hers. "I've wanted you since the minute I laid eyes on you." He hesitated and his voice grew soft. "But if *you're* not ready, I can wait."

"Really?"

Her voice had a husky quality, nearly bringing him to his knees. He nodded, took her hand in his and brought it to his mouth, placing a gentle kiss against her palm. All the time she watched with those huge chocolate eyes. His body began to stir once again. "Now, don't go looking at me that way," he began, "or I'll forget all my good intentions and I'll be all over you again." Lafe knew Michelle was still scared. Hell! He was scared, too.

"Maybe if we take it slow," she suggested timidly. "I'm worried about our relationship at the site. What will the men think?"

"I don't give a damn what people think, but if it bothers you..." With any other woman, if she didn't play by his rules, Lafe would just say goodbye and be out the door. This time it was different. He wanted more; he wanted Michelle with such a need that he didn't know if it would be satisfied with one night in bed.

The next morning, Michelle checked on T.J., and was pleased with his quick recovery. They finished their chores from Saturday, then gathered their beach clothes and headed for Newport Beach. It was about noon when she pulled her Volkswagen into the driveway and saw Lafe coming out the door to greet them. Her heart leaped when she saw his smiling face. He jogged to the car in a pair of white shorts and a blue T-shirt. His feet were bare.

Although it had been less than twelve hours since she had last seen him, she was still hungry for the sight of him. She remembered how Lafe had held her in his arms...how he'd kissed her...how he'd... *Oh, boy, I have to stop thinking this way if I want to survive the day,* she told herself.

"Lafe, I brought my new boogie board," T.J. called out. "Do you know how to surf?"

Lafe leaned his forearm against the open car door. "I've never tried. Is it hard?"

"Nah, it's easy," the child said as he climbed out of the VW. "Uncle Joe taught me last year, and I was only six." He reached behind the seat and pulled out his colorful soft board.

"Hmmm...I don't know."

T.J. looked up at Lafe, holding on to a surfboard that was nearly twice his size. "I can show you how."

Lafe squatted next to the boy. "Well, we can give it a try. Now, why don't you go inside and change, while I help your mother bring in the other things." T.J. took off and Lafe turned his attention to Michelle.

"Hi." He came around the car. "I missed you."

"I missed you, too," she confessed shyly, and his mouth closed over hers. Michelle wrapped her arms around him, enjoying the feel of his warmth. Finally he released her, but kept his arm across her shoulders.

"Lafe, can I ask a favor?"

He kissed the end of her nose. "Sure. Anything."

"I don't want T.J. to know about us yet." She saw his confusion and rushed to explain. "I haven't dated anyone since Tom's death, and I don't know how he'll handle it." *And I'm scared that we'll both get hurt when you leave,* she cried to herself.

There was a long pause as the muscles in his jaw tightened. "I don't like sneaking around, Michelle, not even for the so-called sake of the kids."

Michelle knew Lafe well enough to realize that he would never do anything to hurt T.J. intentionally, but she still had to protect her son. "What about after you're gone?"

"That doesn't mean I'm going to drop off the end of the earth, or never see you and T.J. again."

Michelle wanted to believe him, but life for her son had been filled with disappointments. T.J. was so trusting and vulnerable when it came to loving. He was a lot like his mother.

"Will you at least give me a few days and let me tell him?"

Lafe's expression was dark, brooding. "I'm still not crazy about the idea, but I'll give you time."

Michelle hugged him. "Thank you."

After changing into her swimsuit, Michelle walked down to the beach to join the others. Her plan was to park herself on the sand and relax in the afternoon sun. Today she'd decided against her yellow bikini and opted for a more conservative one-piece, blue-and-violet striped suit.

"Hey, Mom," T.J. yelled as he rode belly down on his boogie board.

Shading her eyes from the sun, Michelle stretched out on a towel. She watched Lafe come out of the ocean. His broad chest and shoulders glistened with beads of water; as the water ran down his lithe torso, it caught in the swirling hair that narrowed into his dark boxer-style trunks. His tanned skin was now nearly bronze. He looked more like a California native than a Colorado cowboy. All and all Lafe was one devastatingly good-looking man. He sure got her pulse racing.

Lafe brushed the wet hair from his face and lay down next to her. "I liked that cute bikini you had on yesterday, but I think I love this one," he remarked as his eyes traveled the length of her body.

"So do I."

"I didn't like the way the men were ogling you."

"I noticed you had quite a crowd around you, too, namely one Carrie Stafford."

"Jealous?"

She rolled over onto her stomach and pillowed her head on her folded arms. "Hardly."

"C'mon, Michelle. Carrie's a kid." Lafe took out the suntan lotion, squeezed some out in his hand and began rubbing it onto the backs of her legs. Her body tingled as his fingers erotically moved slowly up and down her calves. "I'm thirteen years older than she is."

"I don't think she was counting," she stressed, trying to concentrate on the conversation and not on his hands, which were traveling upward to her thighs.

"You should talk, the way Lawson was hanging around you."

"Chris and I are friends. Besides, I had nothing to do with that. But I think Betty had a hand in the attention we both were getting."

"Who cares?" He smiled. "It ended up the way I wanted...well almost." He reached over and gave her a quick kiss.

Michelle's glance flew to the water as she tried to determine if T.J. had seen them. "Lafe, you promised," she whispered.

"You're just too tempting, and I'm too...hot." He stood and carried her with him. "Let's go for a swim."

Michelle gasped, her hands pushing against his chest, her legs kicking in the air. "Lafe, put me down."

"Oh, and who's going to make me?" He laughed as he strode into the surf.

T.J. cheered as his mother was deposited in the ocean.

Michelle stood up, sputtering at the feel of the waist-high water. After she'd lain in the warm sun, the water was freezing. "All right, Mr. Colter. Say your prayers," she warned, "because you're going to get it this time."

"Yeah, and just what are you going to give me?" Lafe tossed her a sexy grin, folding his arms across his chest, letting his gaze travel the length of her suit.

Michelle glanced down at her wet nylon suit. It clung to her body and left nothing to the imagination. Michelle groaned and swiftly dived into the surf, swimming out to deeper water.

Lafe followed close behind, finally catching up to her. He grabbed her waist and pulled her to him. "Michelle, slow down."

"Lafe, don't." She looked around for T.J.

"Stop worrying. T.J. went into the house to get something to drink."

"How convenient for you," she teased.

"All I wanted was a little time alone with you." His arms encircled her waist, bringing her closer. "That's better." Lafe sighed as his hands moved along her back and across her hips.

Michelle gasped. "Oh, Lafe we're not supposed to be doing this." She sucked in a breath as her body arched to meet his touch.

"You're wrong—we should be doing this and more." His head dipped under the mild surf and he placed his mouth over her taut nipple. Michelle bit back a moan, and somehow found the strength to push Lafe away and swim toward the beach and T.J. It would be safer if the three of them stayed together.

It was almost five before T.J. and Lafe had finally had enough of the ocean. Michelle couldn't believe how much energy they both had after spending hours in the water, and they were also hungry. Luckily Lafe's refrigerator was well stocked. Michelle offered to cook the hamburgers if he started the grill. Then she ran upstairs to change.

After a quick shower, she dressed, then went into Lafe's bedroom to get T.J.'s clothes off the bed. She didn't want her son dragging sand into the house, so she had him use the outside shower. The room was Ben and Mary's, and it came with a king-size bed and a big picture window with a great view of the ocean. As she glanced at the ivory-colored down comforter, her heart turned over. If she'd accepted Lafe's invitation at the party to come home with him last night, she could have woken up in this bed . . . in Lafe's arms.

Michelle swiftly dismissed the thought. She'd never been the type to indulge in a . . . a purely physical relationship. That wasn't quite true, she reminded herself. She had shamefully gone after Lafe in Colorado. Her breath quickened as she recalled last night on her sofa and how fast things had gotten out of hand once again. There wasn't any doubt that she wanted Lafe, and he wanted her. But for how long? she wondered. Another six weeks, until the project was completed?

Michelle was already in love with the man. She glanced at her watch. As of July 16, at 5:23 p.m., there hadn't been any sort of declaration from Lafe. Could she really expect one? She knew he planned on retiring and going back to his ranch.

She walked to the bed and gathered up T.J.'s clothes. Then, seeing Lafe's tennis shorts on the floor, she smiled. She picked them up, too, and his wallet fell out of the pocket. Retrieving it, she found herself staring at her son's Little League picture. She smiled, knowing that T.J. must have given it to him. Unable to resist the temptation, she glanced through the other clear plastic holders, only to see credit cards. No other pictures adorned his wallet. She knew that Lafe was an only child. His uncle, the only family he'd had, had passed away.

She hugged herself to ease the ache in her chest, wondering about all the holidays and birthdays. Did he spend them alone? Suddenly she was overcome with her own loneliness as she remembered her ten-year marriage and the all-too-vivid pain of loving someone who hadn't really loved her back. Michelle had learned that the only way to protect herself was not to let herself care for anyone.

Tears rushed into her eyes. It was too late. She already did care . . . too much.

Lafe sensed Michelle's mood when she came downstairs. The playful and laughing woman who'd shown up hours earlier had disappeared. He didn't know what had caused the change in mood, but he was going to find out. Just as soon as he got T.J. settled in front of the TV with a movie. It was still early, but Michelle wasn't easily persuaded to stay. Before he and T.J. ran out to the video store both had to do a lot of promising to finish the dishes and clean up.

Since it was blocking his truck in the driveway, Lafe drove Michelle's VW. Somehow he squeezed into the small car, and with T.J. seated next to him, they went to the neighborhood video-rental store. Twenty minutes later they'd chosen a half-dozen movies that would hold a seven-year-old's interest, so that Lafe could spend some time with Michelle.

On the drive back to the beach house, T.J. grew quiet. Lafe figured it was because the boy was tired, until he finally asked, "Do you think my mom is pretty?"

Lafe was taken aback. "Yes, I think she's very pretty."

"Do you like her?" The boy wrinkled his nose. "I mean like on TV when a man and woman kiss and stuff."

"Yes," Lafe answered honestly, smiling but not forgetting Michelle's request to keep things quiet.

"Do you—"

"Hold it, T.J." Lafe held up his hand. "I think we've been friends long enough that you can say what's on your mind, don't you?"

T.J.'s face reddened. "Well, I saw you kissing her when you were in the water." His eyes widened. "I wasn't snooping—really. I just looked out the kitchen window and saw you."

"It's okay, son. I care a lot about your mother."

Momentarily looking away from the road, Lafe glanced at the boy sitting beside him. He didn't seem happy. "I take it you're not crazy about the idea."

"My dad used to yell at Mom a lot and she'd cry...." The boy swallowed hard, then his voice softened to a whisper. "I could hear her at night from my bedroom."

Lafe gripped the steering wheel, knowing T.J. had probably received the same treatment from Tom Royer. Lafe knew all too well what it was like to be resented, not able to do anything right, trying so hard to please. How many nights did a little boy have to cry himself to sleep? He pulled the car into the driveway at the house and parked, but didn't get out. He turned in his seat and leaned against the door.

"T.J., I care a lot about you and your mom. And I promise never to hurt her or you the way your father did."

Although T.J.'s head was lowered, Lafe could see the child nod. Lafe reached over, put his arm across the boy's shoulders and pulled T.J. into a tight embrace. The child hugged him around the middle.

"I wish you were my dad," the boy whispered.

Lafe squeezed him tighter and found himself thinking about the same thing. They sat there for a moment, then finally Lafe held T.J. at arm's length to look at him.

"T.J.," he began, "what we talked about here is between us. Your mother and I have some things to work out." Lafe watched the boy nod again. "But if she's agrees, I'd like you both to visit my ranch before you start school this fall. She and I should be finished with the project by then."

T.J.'s head popped up. "Oh, wow! Really?"

Lafe smiled. "Yes, but remember it's a secret. Your mother has to be the one who decides to go."

"I'll be really good, Lafe. I promise. I won't do anything bad."

"I know, son," Lafe murmured, a catch in his voice. He knew this child couldn't be bad if he tried.

"Will you teach me how to ride a horse?"

"I was plannin' on it. But first we'd better get you a hat."

"Oh, wow!"

After dinner Michelle stood out on the patio, watching the clouds play peekaboo with the moon. A cool breeze raised goose bumps on her arms, but she was feeling too peaceful to go inside. She turned around and saw Lafe coming through the sliding-glass door. He had a sweater thrown over his arm and in his hands were two mugs.

She smiled, took the sweater and put it on. Then he offered her the coffee.

"Thought you might be getting lonely...and maybe a little cold."

"You cowboys are so perceptive. Thanks." She took a sip and rested the cup on the railing.

"Ah, shucks, ma'am. Just tryin' to be neighborly." He leaned down and placed a gentle kiss on her mouth. Michelle immediately melted into his body, loving his warmth, his strength ... his everything. At that moment she couldn't think of anything she didn't love about this man.

Finally Lafe broke off the kiss with a soft groan. "I've been wanting to do that for hours."

"Well, little people have big eyes."

"Right now your little person has his big eyes on *The Great Muppet Caper.*"

"Good." She loved the way Lafe had taken time to be with her son. He had made the whole weekend wonderful, but she had to think about returning to reality. "We should be heading for home."

"Bite your tongue, woman." Lafe drew his hand across the curve of her hips, pressing her closer. "I'm not letting you go, not for hours yet."

Michelle closed her eyes and looped her arms around his neck. "Lafe, I can't stay. We have to be at the site by eight in the morning."

He shifted his body against hers, making her keenly aware of the fact that he wanted her. "Will I have to go back to calling you 'Ms. Royer' tomorrow?"

She smacked him playfully, trying to break the sexual tension between them. "You've never called me that."

He placed another heated kiss on her lips, and she trembled.

"How about I call you 'honey'? 'Sweetheart'? 'Baby'? 'Love muffin'?"

"No, please," Michelle begged as she began to laugh. "How about just calling me 'Michelle.' "

She lifted her head and looked up at him. All amusement on his face was gone. "How about I just call you 'my woman'?"

Chapter Eleven

The next morning, Lafe made it to the site before Michelle...hours before, almost beating the sunrise. He had some thinking to do, and being at the beach house, where he and Michelle had spent the previous day, didn't help his concentration.

She'd made a quick departure the night before, right after he'd teasingly called her "my woman." One minute they were joking, and the next she was walking out the door. He'd thought about phoning her, but because of the late hour, he hadn't wanted to disturb her sleep. She had ruined any hope he might have had for a restful night. A long, exhausting run on the beach hadn't helped, and by morning he had felt like hell. The woman was tearing him apart.

All those years he had guarded and protected himself, not getting close to anyone so he wouldn't get hurt. Well, that defense didn't work anymore, since Michelle had come along and blindsided him.

Now, as Lafe approached the trailer, he took a deep breath. He needed to get to work so he could finish this damn project and get the hell out of California...and on with his life. He sat down behind his desk, picked up the phone and began to dial the number of his injured roofing contractor, cursing because there was one more delay that would keep him on the job.

He was leaning back in his chair when the door opened and Michelle walked in. He noticed the dark circles under her eyes. She hadn't slept any better than he had.

"Lafe, can we discuss the crew working—"

"No!" he interrupted as he stood up. "We need to talk about what happened last night. Why did you leave so suddenly?"

She looked everywhere but at him. "It was late. I needed to get home."

He hissed out a long breath. "C'mon, Michelle, you nearly ran out the door. If I said or did something, don't you owe me the courtesy of telling me?"

He watched as Michelle shut her eyes, then after a moment she opened them again. "I'm not your woman, Lafe. You don't own me." She raised her chin stubbornly. "No man will ever control me again."

He gave a incredulous laugh as he came around the desk. "God, Michelle, we were kidding around. I thought you knew that. I never meant . . ."

Michelle had spent a lot of time deciding whether or not she should take a chance. She was crazy about this man, but she would never lose herself again. "I might be overly cautious, but I can't take the chance of getting hurt again."

Lafe searched her face, as if trying to read her thoughts. Then he came forward and drew her into his arms. "Ssh, Michelle. I'd never hurt you. Don't you think you can trust me?"

She glanced away from his intense gaze. "I needed a little time to come to terms with my feelings."

He moved toward her and gripped her by the arms. "And . . ."

"And I realized that I do trust you, too—"

Before she could finish, Lafe had gathered her up in a tight embrace.

"Oh, Michelle! I was so afraid that I'd lost you." He pulled back slightly, then covered her mouth in a hot, hungry kiss.

It was like an electric shock, and Michelle made a purring sound and surrendered to the urgency crying out in her. Her mouth softened beneath his; she was desperate for the taste of him. Lafe shifted his hold, bringing her closer. She couldn't do any more than just cling to him, feeling as if she were drowning in the wonderful sensations he created in her.

A shudder rocked Lafe and he tore his mouth away, his breathing labored in the silent room.

"I ... I was going to suggest we take it slow." She pulled out of the embrace and was surprised when Lafe released her so easily.

"It's been hot since the minute we met," he confessed as he took another steadying breath. Their eyes met and he reached down and kissed the corner of her mouth. "It's never been like this for me. . . . Ever."

"It's never been this way for me, either."

He grinned as he started to reach for her, but Michelle dodged his grasp.

"Lafe, we have to talk." Smiling, she raised her hand in defense, but he grabbed it and brought her up against him. "We can't mix our personal lives with the business."

"Why? We can work together."

"What about the men? I'm the brunt of enough of their jokes as it is. I want to be taken seriously."

"C'mon, Michelle, only a few of the crew don't take you seriously. Everyone else thinks you're doing a fine job. And that includes me.

She smiled. "Thanks, I needed to hear that." She raised up on her toes and offered him a sweet kiss, but Lafe had other ideas.

He opened his mouth over hers and Michelle shuddered as his tongue dived into her, stroking, teasing and taunting in a way that made her forget everything but this man she loved so desperately.

"Good, I'm glad to see the two of you getting along so well."

They tore themselves apart and jumped back, to see Jeff smiling at them.

"Dammit, Jeff." Lafe looked just as embarrassed as Michelle felt. "Can't you at least knock and let someone know you're around?"

The foreman's gaze darted back and forth between the two of them. He grinned. "Well, from the looks of it, in the future I guess I'm going to have to."

For the next few weeks things went smoothly with Ocean Bluff. And even though Lafe complained, Michelle made sure that he stayed away from her at the site. They spent evenings and weekends together, but they both discovered that there was never enough time.

Michelle usually cooked, but Lafe was always there to help. Even T.J. pitched in. It was like a family, the way Michelle had always wanted things to be. But deep in the back of her mind, she knew that Ocean Bluff was Lafe's last job. He would be returning to Colorado. Everything she treasured was in Southern California, including the family she loved. Her job with Stafford Investments that gave her a feeling of independence and self-worth. She knew that if she wanted Lafe, it was going to be on his terms. She also knew that she couldn't give up everything for a man again. Not even Lafe Colter.

Of course, Lafe hadn't mentioned anything permanent. Maybe he never would. Then she wouldn't have anything to worry about, except a broken heart. Right now her immediate concern was completing Ocean Bluff. They still hadn't caught the thieves who'd been robbing the site, and Lafe was spending his nights in the trailer again.

"I don't like you being here all night." Michelle glanced at Lafe. "What if these guys have guns?"

"We have security guards, Michelle. But Jeff and I are still going to hang around to help out. Believe me, I'm not so macho that I'd endanger my life over a few fixtures."

Lafe knew that Michelle wasn't convinced. And he loved the fact that she was concerned about his safety. It had been a long time since anyone had cared about him.

"I have a feeling these guys are amateurs. If only we can figure out how they're getting in and stealing from us." He pulled her into his arms, hugging her close. "Why don't you go home? You look beat."

"That's because I can't get enough sleep." She raised her head off his chest. "There's this guy who keeps me up late."

Lafe cocked an eyebrow. "Is that a complaint?"

"Never," she breathed, letting his lips settle on hers. Then he released her with only a tease of what she really wanted.

"You go home and stop worrying about me." He pushed her toward the door. "Worry about finding us some roofing materials. Plus our roofing contractor is no longer able to do the job. It seems we have a little problem here." He looked at her. "Got any ideas, lady?"

Later that night, Michelle was at home going over her list of subcontractors to see if she'd overlooked anyone. She and Lafe had been trying frantically all week to find someone. The last thing they needed at this stage was a delay. Ten parcels had been sold, and the buyers were expecting to take possession in thirty days.

She got on the phone and dialed Ben Stafford's home phone number. She rarely called her boss after-hours, but she knew that he would want to know the situation.

The next morning Michelle walked into the trailer expecting to find Lafe asleep on the sofa. Instead he was busy on the phone and looked as though he'd had a good eight hours' sleep. She was a little disappointed, because she couldn't enjoy waking him up with kisses.

Lafe hung up the phone. "Got great news." He gave her a quick hug.

Michelle's eyes lit up. "You caught the guys who've been stealing from us?"

"No, they've been laying pretty low lately. But I did find a contractor and he can get us the roofing materials."

"Great!" Her enthusiasm ebbed. "When?"

"Monday morning. There's a catch, though. It's going to cost us more." He picked up the scratch pad with his figures on it from his desk and handed it to her.

Michelle's eyes widened. "Lafe, this is an increase of twenty percent. And this material isn't what we'd originally ordered."

"It's damn close. Just a different manufacturer. Besides, it would take three weeks before we got our original order. Maybe longer." He gave her a wry smile. "And if we wait, what do we tell the families who plan on moving in by then?"

Michelle wasn't happy about this whole new development. "I think we should wait."

"C'mon, Michelle. We don't have that luxury. Harry said that he has to know no later than today, so he can get us the materials by Monday."

"Who is Harry?"

"Harry Travis, the subcontractor."

Harry Travis. Michelle swallowed hard. She remembered the name well and it hadn't been on the list she'd given Lafe. For good reason. Other contractors had let it slip that he took kickbacks. Michelle didn't want him working on Ocean Bluff.

"I don't want him on this project."

"Why?"

"Because he takes kickbacks."

Lafe folded his arms across his chest. "That's an allegation or has it ever been proven?"

Michelle nervously looked away. "No, but...his bid is still too high."

"Not now it isn't," Lafe challenged. "We've come in pretty close to cost on this project. But dammit, Michelle! We need to spend the extra money to guarantee completion on time. And so far Travis is the only one willing to do that for us."

"I won't use him."

Lafe couldn't deal with Michelle's stubbornness. He'd had a long talk with Harry Travis after he'd gone over the subcontractor's list, looking for someone who could provide the materials. The man needed the work and they needed roofs put on. "Well, it's my job to hire the subcontractor. And I'm going to offer him—"

"I don't think so," Michelle interrupted. "I'm still the project manager. I have the final say. And I won't authorize that amount of money."

"I'll go to Ben."

Michelle's stomach tightened. Her hands began to tremble, and she prayed to God Lafe wouldn't notice. She couldn't believe that he would go over her head. But what did she expect from a man? They had to let you know that they were in control. Well, she wasn't going to let him get away with it.

"Fine. Do what you feel you need to do." She started across the room, then paused at the door. "It just seems strange to me that Harry Travis is the only subcontractor in the area you can get for the job," she said. "He's going to be making out like a bandit. At our expense." *And at the expense of our relationship,* she thought, feeling betrayed.

Now was not the time for regrets. Lafe had made his choice and she had to make hers. She walked out of the trailer, slamming the door resoundingly behind her.

The tears started the minute Michelle had climbed in the car, and she hadn't been able to stop them the entire twenty minutes it had taken her to get to the office. No one was going to tell her how to do her job.

Michelle parked her car and looked in the mirror as she wiped away the last of her tears, hoping no one would notice she'd been crying. Climbing out the driver's seat, she headed toward the building. On the ride up the elevator, she began rehearsing what she was going to say to Ben, and by the time she got off on her floor, she was more than ready to argue her position.

Carol Martin, Ben's secretary, greeted her with a friendly inquiry, but Michelle wasn't in the mood to talk. The woman sensed it and told her Ben was free to see her. Michelle thanked her and walked into the large walnut-paneled office, where she found her boss working at his desk.

"Ben?" She didn't want to disturb him, but this was important.

He looked up and smiled. "Michelle. Come in." He got up. "I was expecting you. Lafe just called."

"What? He called you already?" She was furious. "Did he explain what's been going on?"

Ben sighed as he took off his glasses. "Yes, he told me about the delay in getting the roofing materials. He said they aren't going to be able to ship them until close to the end of the month."

"Is that all?" Michelle couldn't believe her ears. "Didn't he tell you about the roofing subcontractor he found this morning?"

Ben shook his head. "No, he never mentioned anyone. Maybe he decided not to use him."

"Yeah, maybe...."

"Now, about the delay...? We should still be able to finish pretty close to deadline if we work around the roofing problem. I'll contact the families personally and see if they'll be inconvenienced by the setback." Ben began to smile. "I'll even offer to put them up at the Marriott here in Newport Beach. That should keep them happy for a few days. What do you think?"

She began to smile along with her boss. "I think it's a great idea."

Ben grew serious. "Now, Michelle, you have to guarantee me that the materials will get here without another delay."

"Believe me, Ben, I've talked to the supplier nearly every day this past week. Three weeks tops. If there's a problem I'll climb up on the roof myself and help finish the job," she promised as she started for the door, then heard Ben call to her.

"Michelle, if I haven't told you lately, you're doing a terrific job. When this is over, I owe you a night on the town."

She smiled her thanks.

"It's just too bad about the thefts at the site." Ben frowned. "I hate the thought of Lafe staying out there at night, but, he says it's his job." Ben sat on the edge of his desk, and his gaze met Michelle's. "You don't find many men like Lafe Colter these days. He takes each and every job seriously, which is as it should be. He has worked hard to build a fine reputation in Colorado and now in California."

Michelle swallowed the lump in her throat. "I know, Ben. He's a fine man." She couldn't stay any longer or she would break down. "I've got to get back."

She hurried out the door and to the elevator. She smiled tentatively as hope welled in her heart. Maybe Lafe was different . . . maybe there was a chance for them after all.

"Jeff, you go home and get some sleep. I'll call you around four so you can relieve me," Lafe said, trying to get his foreman out the door.

He wasn't in the mood for company tonight. And he wasn't in the mood for any questions. Not after today. He glanced up to see his friend staring at him.

"What's the matter?"

"That's what I want to know," Jeff said. "I saw Michelle run out of here yesterday and she looked about as miserable as you do. Did you two have a fight?"

"It's none of your business."

"I'm making it my business," the foreman countered. Jeff knew he was about the only person Lafe would let get away with talking like that to him.

"Hey, I'm just in a bad mood. This project has been hell." Lafe sighed, hoping Jeff was buying it. "Thank God this is my last."

"If you say so." Jeff didn't look convinced as he gathered up his things and headed for the door. "Just make sure you call and wake me."

Lafe waved in agreement as Jeff start to walk out, but stopped and moved aside, allowing Michelle to come into the trailer. Lafe's pulse raced as he watched the two exchange a friendly greeting, then Jeff left. Lafe couldn't think of a single excuse to bring his foreman back. But he didn't need to be alone with Michelle.

His gaze traveled the length of the woman who tore at his heart. She was dressed in a pair of black stretch pants and a turtleneck. Her hair was pulled back and tied into a ponytail. She looked nervous and about fifteen years old, which made his thoughts very much illegal.

"What are you doing here?"

She studied him for a moment, then her gaze darted around the room. "I...I came to thank you, and to help keep watch.

"You're welcome. Now, go home where it's safe."

She lifted her chin. "I'm staying, Lafe. I have as much at stake in catching the thief as you do."

Lafe moved behind his desk and pulled the window blind shut so the office light wouldn't be seen outside, then he sat down in his chair. "Fine, you want to hang around, hang around. It doesn't bother me. Just don't leave the trailer," he warned. "I don't want to have to worry about your safety, too."

"You don't have to worry about me. I can take care of myself."

"Well, it's a little late—" He stopped and drew in a long, frustrating breath.

Michelle stood her ground on the other side of the desk. She didn't want to get too close to Lafe and weaken her defenses. They needed to work out this problem on a professional level. "You had no right to tell me you'd go over my head."

Lafe shrugged. "I've done it before on a job," he admitted. "But when I thought about it, you had good reasons not to want to use my subcontractor."

"My, aren't we generous." She walked the length of the trailer, as far away from Lafe as possible, and stopped in front of the other desk.

"Okay, maybe I did get a little angry, too," he admitted.

She turned around and raised an eyebrow. "A little?"

"All right, a lot," he corrected. "Want anything else from me? How about some blood?"

He acted as if he were teasing, but his eyes told her differently.

"Why is it so difficult for men to give women any credit?" she began. "I already knew of Travis's reputation, but you acted like I was the bad guy."

"That's not true," Lafe denied. "Didn't I call Ben and tell him we were going to wait until the original supplier delivered the material?"

"Yes, but after we fought and I called your bluff."

"C'mon, Michelle. We argued over a difference of opinion. It's only a job."

She clenched her hands into fists. "No," she stated, wondering what it took to get through to this man. "Ocean Bluff may be only another job to you, but it's *my* career that's on the line here." *And my self-esteem and independence,* she added silently.

"Ocean Bluff is not just a job, but it's not more important than what's happening between us." He stood up.

"No, but it's part of me, Lafe. You can't have one without the other."

Cursing, Lafe turned away and ran his fingers through his hair. "Dammit, Michelle! It shouldn't matter."

"Lafe, I can't give up everything. Not again. Once I let a man manipulate me into thinking that I couldn't do anything for myself." Her glare challenged him. "I spent ten years in that prison."

"I'm not Tom, Michelle. I'd never try to take away your independence."

Lafe knew his words were a waste of time. He wasn't getting through to her. No matter what he said, Michelle wasn't going to believe him. But he kept on trying. "Can't we put this project aside for a few minutes and talk about us? We need to separate it from our personal lives."

"But how can we?" she asked. "It's part of us."

"Not if we don't make it." He moved to put his arm around her, and when she didn't pull away, he hugged her against him. "Everyone needs time out, especially us." He kissed her forehead and she relaxed in his arms.

"We have to finish Ocean Bluff," she insisted.

"It will get finished," he promised. "But we're letting it consume everything. I want time for us."

She looked up at him. "I do, too. You'll be going back to Colorado before long and—"

Lafe's mouth closed over hers. He didn't wait for her to finish. Too many times words had caused them problems. He pulled her closer, wrapping her in a tight embrace, savoring the feel of her against him. Finally he broke off the kiss and began nibbling his way to the sensitive spot below her ear.

"You don't have to miss me, Michelle. Come back to Colorado with me."

Her eyes filled with excitement. "Lafe, I can't just go off..."

He bit back a smile. "Lady, this isn't an indecent proposal. This is a real one. Marry me. I want you and T.J. to come live with me at the ranch."

"Lafe..." she breathed. "What about my family?"

"They can visit."

Michelle's heart pounded uncontrollably as she moved out of his embrace. It all sounded too wonderful, Lafe wanting to marry her. T.J. would have a real father, she would have...

"C'mon, Michelle, you're making me nervous. What do you say?"

"But my job..." *What about love?*

"You don't need to work. I've worked hard enough the past fifteen years for all of us to live comfortably. I want you at home with me."

Michelle felt her heart sink as his words echoed in her head. "Lafe, that's not fair. I enjoy what I do, and I want to continue doing it."

Lafe drew a long breath. "But why, if you don't have to?"

"Because I want to. Just as you wanted to build a business fifteen years ago. Mainly, I like to be able to make my own decisions."

Lafe felt the pain of Michelle's rejection everywhere. He knew that she might marry him if he stayed in the business. But he couldn't. Work had consumed his life for too long, and he needed out. "Then I guess you'd better make one now."

He watched as tears clouded her eyes. "Can't you stay here and continue to work for Ben?"

"I can't, Michelle. As much as I . . . care about you and T.J., I just can't."

"And I can't let a man control my life." She stepped back from him. "I won't live that way again. I can't, Lafe. I just can't." Abruptly she spun around and all but ran out the door.

Lafe hurried outside, surprised to find that Michelle had taken off in the direction of the bluff. He tore after her, catching up with her about halfway there. He managed to grab her arm and swing her around.

"Running away won't solve anything, Michelle."

She fought him, trying to jerk out of his hold. "Just leave me alone."

Lafe thought about doing just that, until he spotted the two figures coming up the bluff. He pushed Michelle into the high grass and covered her body with his to hold her down.

"Lafe, what are you doing?"

"Quiet. There are two men out there. And unless I miss my guess, they're the ones stealing from us."

Michelle's attention turned to where Lafe pointed. She saw two dark forms about fifty feet away and heading for the site. "Well, let's get them."

"We will, but first we need proof," he said as he rolled off her and pulled a walkie-talkie from his belt. He jerked up the antenna and pressed the button. "Jack, it's Lafe. Do you copy? Over."

After a few seconds an answer came. "Yeah, Lafe. What's up? Over."

"I spotted two guys coming toward the site from the bluff side. If my guess is right, they're the ones we're looking for. They're headed for the supply pen. Over."

"I'll take some men and get over there. Over."

"Wait, Jack. Give them a few minutes. I want these two caught with their hands on the merchandise. Over."

"Gotcha. Over."

Lafe put away his walkie-talkie and climbed to his feet. "C'mon, you're going back to the trailer." To his surprise, Michelle obediently followed him until she was safely inside. "No matter what, keep this door locked until I come back." He turned and left.

Michelle paced the room for what seemed like hours, until finally she heard Lafe's voice. She opened the door and was greeted by several people, including the two handcuffed suspects. To her shock they were Bill and Larry, the carpenters she had hired for the project. She tried to get Lafe's attention to see if he was okay, but he was only interested in making a phone call to the local police.

Nearly an hour later the two men had been read their rights and were on their way to the police station in a patrol car. Jack, the security guard, went along, and Lafe told them he'd be there shortly.

Once they were alone, Lafe turned to Michelle. "Well, it looks like it's finally over."

Michelle's hands began shake. She knew he meant more than just the robberies. "I guess it is. Maybe now we can finish this project without any more problems."

"That would be nice," he said.

There was an unspoken pain in his eyes, and her own emotions clogged her throat. She tried hard to hide how desperately she needed him. But when Lafe looked at her with longing, she was powerless to resist. He walked to her, gathered her into his arms as his mouth lowered to hers.

Michelle couldn't stop her reaction any more than her next breath. She loved this man. She raised her arms to encircle his neck and deepened their kiss, wanting it never to end but knowing their time together was soon going to be a fleeting memory. She opened her mouth and his tongue greeted hers, causing her to purr from the sheer pleasure.

Lafe tore his mouth away. They were both breathing raggedly. His brilliant sea green eyes were fixed on her, as if he were trying to memorize her face. He raised his hand and stroked her cheek.

"I guess it's like it was in Glenwood Springs. Once again our timing is all wrong." He squeezed his eyes shut for a moment, then he opened them. "Goodbye, Michelle." He walked out of the trailer door and out of her life.

Chapter Twelve

Ben Stafford had a big grin on his face as he looked around the site. "I can't believe it," he said as he turned to Lafe. "Ocean Bluff is completed."

"Whoa, Ben." Lafe raised his hand. "It's *nearly* completed. As you can see the roofers won't be finished until tomorrow, and the landscapers are coming back at the end of the week to lay the final strips of sod for the lawns."

"I don't care. It's close enough," Ben stated as he once again studied the area.

Lafe, too, took a good look at the Cape Cod-style homes against the beautiful and serene backdrop of the Pacific Ocean. This wasn't as joyous a moment for Lafe, though, as he recalled the past month of the project.

He had been determined to finish this job on time, no matter what it took. He needed to get on with his life, even if it was going to be a dismal existence without Michelle. The sooner he got back to the ranch permanently the better for everyone.

"I wish I could talk you into staying in the business awhile longer." Ben's words broke into Lafe's thoughts. "After these beauties, you could probably write your own ticket here in California.''

''Thanks, Ben. But I've been there. It's time for a change.''

Ben gave him a sideways glance. ''I have a feeling that you'll be getting bored with only cattle to keep you company.'' His friend suddenly looked startled. ''Lafe, I'm sorry. I didn't mean to bring up...''

Lafe forced a smile. Even though he'd never come out and said anything, he knew that Ben was aware of his relationship with Michelle, as was the entire office. ''It's okay. Sometimes things aren't meant to work out.'' *Like my life,* he thought. All he wanted now was to go back to the ranch. Things had to get better.

''Ben, I need a favor.''

''Anything.''

''I don't like to ask this, but since there's only a little finish-up work on the project, I'd like to put Jeff in charge. I need to get back to the ranch. It's time to think about roundup.'' Actually, Lafe had a few more weeks until then, but hanging around Southern California any longer wasn't going to accomplish anything.

''When do you want to go?''

Lafe drew a tired breath. ''I thought I'd head back tonight.''

''Tonight?'' Ben looked clearly surprised, but gentleman that he was, he covered it well. ''Sure. I would have liked to have you around for the little celebration we've planned, especially since I won't get to see you for a while. But if you need to get back...''

Lafe felt bad that he was running out on his friend. ''You know you and Mary are always welcome at the ranch. I have a huge house with plenty of room. I might even talk you into getting on a horse.''

''I'd like that. Maybe next summer.'' Ben offered his hand to Lafe. ''You take care and keep in touch, son.'' Then the older man pulled him into a hug and slapped him on the back affectionately. ''I hope the ranch is everything you're looking for.''

Lafe's emotions were awfully close to the surface as he broke away from the embrace. He had to keep his eyes averted.

"I thought it was once," he said. "Now I'm not so sure."

"T.J., turn down the television. It's too loud," Michelle called into the family room. "I can't even hear myself think," she murmured to herself. Finally the volume softened.

She sighed. Maybe it was better not to think, since her thoughts immediately went to Lafe. The way he smiled, the way he held her and kissed her... Dropping her pen on the table, she rubbed her eyes. Darn it. The man managed to push his way into her mind even when she was paying her bills. She glanced down at the large balance in her checking account, silently thanking Ben for his generous bonus.

Michelle leaned back in her chair. With the success of the project, she was on her way now. She had everything she thought she wanted: the security of a good job, and the means and ability to take care of herself and her son. She remembered the promise she'd made on the day she'd buried Tom—not to need, or depend on, anyone again. She had been wrong. Her body ached from the loneliness. The independence she had fought so hard for wasn't comforting anymore.

Suddenly the doorbell chimed and T.J. went tearing through the house, shouting, "I'll get it."

Michelle's heart sank, knowing her son's hopes never faltered. He kept thinking Lafe would be standing on the other side. Michelle stood and followed after him. Maybe she, too, had the same hopes.

T.J. swung the door open, and Betty stood on the porch. "Oh, it's you."

"T.J., that's not nice to say," Michelle reprimanded her son.

"Sorry, Aunt Betty." The child lowered his head. "I was just hoping that... you were someone else."

Betty smiled as she bent to kiss T.J.'s cheek. "It's okay, T.J. I think your mom was, too."

Michelle closed the door as her son went back to the family room.

"The kid's pretty miserable," Betty observed. "And by the looks of it, you aren't doing much better."

"Thanks, Betty, I needed to hear that." Michelle turned and walked back to the dining room table, wishing her friend would refrain from giving her a lecture tonight.

"Lafe's gone."

Michelle swung around. "What do you mean?"

"He left for Colorado tonight."

"What about Ocean Bluff?" How could he leave her when the project wasn't finished?

"Michelle, you know there's not that much to do. Dad said that Jeff will be left in charge."

"But what was his big hurry?"

"C'mon, friend. You can't be that dense." Betty gave her a knowing look. "You turned him down. He had to salvage some of his pride."

Michelle folded her arms across her chest. "Oh, let's not forget a man's pride. We wouldn't want to damage that."

Betty just stood there, shaking her head. "Tom sure did a job on you." Her expression softened. "I'm sorry, Michelle. I wish I could have been around to help. Maybe you wouldn't be so bitter."

Michelle was taken aback by Betty's words. Was she bitter?

"Lafe wanted me to quit my job. And stay at home."

Betty shrugged and said offhandedly, "It's not as bad as it sounds, especially if you have the man of your dreams coming home to you every night. Besides, the last I heard, living on a cattle ranch is work."

Michelle had been miserable this past month. So many times she'd wanted to go to Lafe and tell him she'd play by his rules, but she couldn't. She knew that in the long run she'd be giving away the control she had fought for so hard.

"I think you should remember, Michelle," Betty started again, "you're not the same starry-eyed, eighteen-year-old girl who got married right out of high school—to a boy. Besides, I don't think Tom Royer knew how to love. He couldn't stand it that you weren't dependent on him for everything."

Betty walked to the table and sat down. "Lafe is definitely a man. And you've worked closely with him these past six months. Can you tell me that he's ever tried to control you? On the job or any other time?"

Michelle couldn't look at Betty. She knew everything her friend had said was true. Not once had Lafe resented her or tried to manipulate her. If anything, he had helped her and always stood behind her.

Betty released a long sigh. "My theory is that most men, whether they think it or not, are controlling. It just takes a strong woman to be able to handle a strong man. I have no doubt, Michelle, you can handle one sexy-looking cowboy."

Michelle felt a momentary panic as her mind raced. Was there any possible way...? She glanced at her friend. "Betty, Lafe wants me to stay at home. He doesn't want me to work," she repeated.

"Did he actually say you couldn't work?"

"He said I didn't need to." Michelle shrugged. "Same thing."

"Uh-uh." Betty shook her head. "Maybe he just wants to make things easier for you. I think he wants you to share his life in Colorado." Her friend raised an eyebrow. "Why is this a problem?"

"He never said he loved me."

Betty gave her an incredulous look. "C'mon, the man let you run his construction site and crew the past six months. He got along with your family and treated T.J. as if he were his own. If that isn't love, I don't know what is."

Michelle had trouble taking her next breath. Lafe was in love with her?

"Maybe he was waiting to hear the words from you." Her friend's voice broke through her reverie.

"I guess I never said anything, either," Michelle admitted shyly.

"Don't you think it's about time you did?"

"But I can't just pick up and go after..." She paused. *The man I love,* she thought as her insides did a sudden flip of excitement. She looked at Betty. "You really think I should go to Colorado?"

Betty nodded.

Michelle had more to think about than her own happiness. "T.J. would miss his friends and his grandfather, his uncles—"

"They can visit us at the ranch," her son interrupted.

Michelle swung around, to find T.J. standing in the doorway. How much he had heard she didn't know.

"Lafe said that anyone I wanted to invite could come and stay as long as they wanted."

Michelle exchanged a glance with Betty, then knelt before the forlorn-looking boy. "Honey, that was before. When Lafe and I... When things were different."

"I saw Lafe today. He said he couldn't leave without saying goodbye." T.J. blinked back tears. "He told me that no matter what, he'll always be my friend...yours, too. But he told me not to tell you that because it might make you sad." The child shook his head. "Does it make you sad, Mom?"

Michelle felt her eyes fill with tears, too. "No, T.J., it doesn't make me sad. There are just too many problems between Lafe and me that you wouldn't understand.

"Did he do something bad?" The boy's eyes widened. "Maybe if he says he's sorry, you'll love him again."

"Oh, honey. It's not that. I love Lafe very much."

"Then why did you let him go away?"

Michelle opened her mouth, but she had no answer. She looked at her friend for help.

"Yeah, Michelle. Why'd you let him go away?" Betty repeated.

Michelle blinked in surprise. For the life of her, she didn't know. The problems that she'd thought were between them now seemed so trivial. Love was the important thing, and she knew she had stored up enough for a lifetime.

She stared at her son. "I don't know, T.J. I guess I got scared."

"That's what Lafe said." The small boy laid his hand on her arm as if to comfort her.

Michelle was deeply touched. "What...what else did Lafe say?"

"He said if we ever needed him—" T.J. paused as he began digging into his jeans pocket, then pulled out a piece of paper "—to just call the ranch."

Michelle took the notepaper and recognized Lafe's neat block lettering. It was his address in Durango, Colorado, along with a phone number.

"It seems there aren't any reasons left for not going after what you want." Betty cocked an eyebrow, obviously waiting for Michelle to put up more of a fight.

Michelle ignored her friend's smart remark, knowing she was going to miss her. "T.J., how do you feel about going to Colorado...for a visit?"

The child's eyes rounded. "Oh, wow! I'll go pack my rope."

Lafe tipped his hat off his forehead and eyed the storm clouds rapidly moving in from the north. By tonight they might have their first snow of the season. A little early this year, he thought as he climbed onto the fence railing and looked over a hundred or so bawling calves in the corral. They had another herd of a hundred and fifty in a holding pen behind the barn. He was sure glad they had finished the roundup yesterday. Now all he had left to do was to get the cattle trucked to the stock pens, and he would have the winter to himself.

He jumped down, and started toward the house. Just what he needed, more time to be alone. Not that he hadn't loved working the ranch the past month since he had returned to Durango. But he'd never in his life been so lonely. If it hadn't been for Pete, his foreman, and the two regular ranch hands who resided in the bunkhouse, he probably would have gone completely crazy.

The Double C Ranch wasn't that isolated, but after living in the city for years, it took getting used to again. But it was a trade-off. He had found the peace he needed and had been looking for—he just wished he could have shared it....

Immediately his thoughts went to Michelle. He took off his hat and smacked it against his thigh. He knew that she would never be out of his system or out of his heart. Michelle had been with him every day since his return, whether he had been working the cattle, or just roaming around in the big empty house. At night he lay awake in his big bed and ached from the loneliness.

But things were about to change. Just as soon as he sold off his herd he was going after her. Heading to California, dragging her back to the ranch if he had to. He had to make her understand that they had to at least give themselves a shot at a life together. Dammit! They loved each other.

He'd reached the porch steps when he heard a car coming up the road. He turned to see a faded red Volkswagen Bug cross under the ranch archway and chug up the driveway, literally dying not twenty feet in front of him.

Lafe's heart drummed in his chest, and his breathing was nearly nonexistent when T.J. got out of the car. Then his attention was glued on the driver, as Michelle opened her door and stepped out. He wanted to run to her and take her in his arms, but he found he was unable to move.

It didn't stop his hungry gaze as it roamed over her. She was dressed in a big heavy wine-colored sweater and dark stretch pants that hugged her curves, making him throb from the longing he thought had faded the past month. Her long chestnut hair was swept away from her face and lay in soft curls, making his hand itch to touch them. Then she smiled, and his stomach turned a somersault. God, he had missed her.

"Hello, Lafe."

"Michelle...." He tipped his hat, then he turned to T.J. "Hi, there, partner."

"Hi, Lafe," the boy said shyly, and gave his mother a sideways glance.

"Hey, is that the best I get after you've come all this way?" Lafe held his breath, seeing the boy's sober expression.

Finally T.J. came charging to the porch. "Oh, Lafe, I missed you."

Lafe picked the child up in his arms and hugged him tight. "I missed you more than you'll ever know."

T.J. raised his head. "So you're glad we're here?"

"Real glad." Lafe grinned. "In fact, in a few days I was about to come see you."

The boy's smile disappeared. "Were you going to come and see my mom, too?" he whispered.

"Her especially," Lafe whispered back. "Hey, partner, why don't you head to the barn for a little while." Lafe pointed to the big red building. "Don't go into any stalls. Just holler for Pete and tell him who you are. He'll show you around while your mom and I talk."

T.J. nodded and took off.

Michelle watched her son run off and resisted the temptation to tell him to be careful. She knew that Lafe would never allow T.J. to do anything that would endanger him. He cared too much for him. Did he still care for her, too? She turned back to Lafe.

She had hoped for a warmer welcome—such as Lafe rushing to her and taking her in his arms, telling her how happy he was to see her. The solemn look on his face told her she had a lot of talking to do. Drawing a deep breath, Michelle squared her shoulders and walked toward him. She might as well get started.

"Do you think we could talk?" she asked.

"I'd like that, Michelle." He squinted up into the sky. "In fact, I was a few days off from heading out your way." He looked back at her. "But I'm crazy about the idea that you decided to show up at my door instead," he confessed with a hesitant smile. "Just tell me you didn't come all this way to give me hell for leaving the job early."

She sucked in a long breath as she eyed the worn jeans and scuffed boots. His sheepskin jacket hung open, exposing a plaid flannel shirt. She knew what was underneath the clothes—a muscular chest and a flat stomach.... She shook away the thought.

"No, not about that job, but I do have a proposition for you."

He looked more than disappointed; he looked angry. "If it's about business, I already told you I'm not interested." He turned and headed up the steps.

"No, Lafe." Michelle took off after him, grabbing his arm and managing to turn him around. There was a maddening hint of arrogance in him, and it made her angry. "Listen to me, dammit! If you think I drove all this way just to get lost three times and stay in crummy motels for the last three days, you are sadly mistaken. I put my house up for sale, pulled T.J. out of school, and I feel I deserve a little more than to have you ignore me."

"What?" Lafe's expression softened as his eyes locked with hers. "You're selling your house?"

She nodded.

"You took T.J. out of school? Why?"

Michelle swallowed hard. This wasn't the time to back down. "I... T.J. and I were hoping we had a new home...in Colorado." She looked around at the breathtaking scenery, then up at Lafe. Her heart began hammering in her ears. "Oh, Lafe. If you still want to marry me—"

Michelle didn't get a chance to finish as he gathered her in the circle of his strong arms, taking her mouth in a heated kiss. She felt weak and sagged against him, clinging to the man she loved so urgently that she'd risked her safe, secure life to go after him. Yet they still hadn't settled anything except for the fact that they wanted each other.

Using the last of her willpower, she pushed him away. "Lafe, please, we need to talk. Now."

"What's there to talk about? You're here at the ranch." He started to reach for her again, but she moved back.

"No, first we talk." She began to shake against the cold air. "Maybe we... we can go inside?"

"I'm sorry." Lafe escorted her to the weathered oak door and opened it, allowing her to step inside the large entryway.

She glanced around at the high ceilings, then to the bare hardwood floors. The walls were painted an off-white and accented by a mahogany carved staircase.

"I haven't had much time to work on the inside of the house. This winter I plan to sand down the floors." He looked at her. "I want to leave them bare with just area rugs. What do you think?"

Michelle's breath caught as she grasped any flicker of hope. He wanted her opinion. "Oh, Lafe it's going to look beautiful." She strolled timidly into the living room, to find it devoid of furniture, with only sheer curtains hanging in the windows.

"I got rid of most of my uncle's furniture. Some of the nicer wood pieces I've put upstairs until I'm finished with the floors. C'mon, we can talk in the kitchen."

He led the way and Michelle followed him down the hall. They passed a large paneled room with a desk, which she knew had to be Lafe's office, then they walked through the large dining room where the floors had also been exposed. Finally Lafe pushed open the raised wood door and she found herself inside a dream.

The kitchen was huge, with lots of cabinets, new cabinets in a rich maple color. The countertops were tiled in almond. A round table and six ladder-back chairs sat in the circle of windows overlooking the mountain range.

"This room was in pretty bad shape, so I had the work done the first thing last year." His eyes met hers, but he seemed nervous. "Would you like some coffee?"

Michelle shook her head. "I made a mistake, Lafe."

Silently he leaned against the counter and stared at her.

"We should have tried to work out our problems."

"It's a little difficult when we want different things."

"No, Lafe. We want the same thing." Looking him in the eye, Michelle almost gave up telling him about her idea. "But I want something more. I need to be my own person, independent. I can't let another man take care of me."

When he started to speak she raised her hand. "Just let me finish, because I have a plan that might give us what we both want... and still let us be together."

Lafe wanted to tell her that it didn't matter anymore. He wanted her so desperately that he would do anything to keep her in his life. Because he knew there wasn't any life without Michelle.

"Do you love me?"

She asked so sweetly his emotions nearly choked him. "God, Michelle." He moved toward her. "I love you more than I ever thought possible."

"Oh, Lafe. I love you, too." She smiled at him, but lifted her hand to keep him at a distance. "And I've got a business proposition for you."

Lafe stiffened.

"No," she began, "I don't want you back in the construction business. But I do want to buy your business." She rushed to explain. "That is, Jeff and I want to buy it."

"You've got to be kidding."

"Now...it's not as ridiculous as it sounds. I'll have the money from the sale of my house, and Jeff has savings put away. We can take out a loan for the rest, and...and we'll work right here in Colorado."

Michelle couldn't tell by Lafe's expression what he was thinking. But it didn't stop her from pitching her idea. "And since the construction business in this part of the country is seasonal, I'll only be working during the spring and summer. I can be here, at the ranch, most of the time. Jeff said he knows of several proposed ski resorts in the area that we could put in job bids for." She finally stopped, and looked up at Lafe hopefully. "What do you think?"

"I can't sell you the business, Michelle," he said.

Her heart dropped into her stomach. "Why? Did you already sell it?"

"No, but if you're going to be my wife, everything I have is already yours."

Michelle fought to keep from running into his arms. "Lafe, I have to pay you something."

He gave her a slow, easy grin and she thought she'd never be able to breathe again. "How about a kiss?"

Michelle knew she wasn't going to win this fight, but it didn't matter. She had already won so much.

"So you're saying you'll go along with my idea?"

He nodded. "If you'll go along with marrying me, and you and T.J. live here at the ranch."

Tears filled her eyes as Michelle managed a nod. Her steps were unsteady as she walked into his arms, but she knew that if she stumbled, Lafe would be there for her, not because she was weak, but because he wanted her to be strong. Most of all, because he loved her.

Epilogue

Michelle walked out onto the balcony, and a cool night breeze raised goose bumps on her bare arms as her silky nightgown brushed against her bare skin. She shivered as she leaned against the railing and inhaled the fresh Rocky Mountain air. She loved Glenwood Springs and was happy when Lafe had suggested they get away from the ranch and take a few days off for the honeymoon they'd never had.

Michelle smiled, remembering their wedding day nearly six months earlier in a little church in Durango. Her dad and brothers had flown in, along with Betty and Bill. They'd stayed the rest of the week and celebrated Thanksgiving with the newlyweds. Lafe had suggested they start a tradition and have everyone return the next year.

Christmas had come fast, and although there were only the three of them, they weren't lonely. It was the best Christmas ever. Lafe had gotten T.J. a colt, saying that at seven he was the right age to learn to ride. He had presented her with a new four-wheel-drive vehicle, telling her it was about time she drove a car that was full-size and dependable.

Michelle knew there had been concessions on both sides. Starting up her business took time, even though Jeff did most of the legwork and travel. She didn't always have meals on the table when Lafe walked in the door. He'd told her he didn't mind as long as she was next to him in bed every night. Michelle's body trembled as she remembered Lafe's tender lovemaking. How he'd wanted to please her, making her feel so cherished.

She looked over her shoulder to their bedroom. She felt the blood pounding in her veins in anticipation of being with Lafe. Like every other night since she had met him, she wanted him. She wanted his kisses on her skin; she wanted his hands on her body. . . .

Moving across the wooden deck, Michelle entered the room as Lafe came out of the bathroom. He had a towel wrapped around his waist just as he had two years ago. When he turned, their eyes met, and in the silence they told each other of their need. He held out his arms and she went into his warm embrace.

"I'm glad we came here." She raised her head and kissed his jaw.

"I think we both needed some time alone," Lafe said as he stroked her chin. "There is too much going on at the ranch."

"We needed to get the house finished. And pretty soon the new yearlings will be delivered and you'll be gone more—"

All at once Lafe's mouth covered hers in a searing kiss, and Michelle melted into his body.

"I brought you here, lady, so you could seduce me," he said, finally tearing his mouth from hers.

"Oh, but I tried once. It didn't work," she teased.

Lafe pulled her tight against him. "I guarantee it will this time."

She couldn't help but smile back. "Even if the seducer is pregnant?"

If they were lucky enough to be together for the next fifty years, she would never forget the look on her husband's face. "Are you happy?"

He nodded and she watched tears form in his eyes.

"I thought you wanted to wait."

Michelle found herself blushing. "I discovered that having your baby is the most important thing in the world to me."

He hugged her tight. "No one has ever given me so much as you . . . and T.J." She heard him swallow. "And now a baby . . . I never knew that loving someone could be so wonderful. Not until you, not until you . . . Michelle."

* * * * *

Get Ready to be Swept Away by
Silhouette's Spring Collection

Abduction
& Seduction

These passion-filled stories explore both the dangerous
desires of men and the seductive powers of women.
Written by three of our most celebrated authors, they are
sure to capture your hearts.

Diana Palmer
Brings us a spin-off of her Long, Tall Texans series

Joan Johnston
Crafts a beguiling Western romance

Rebecca Brandewyne
New York Times bestselling author
makes a smashing contemporary debut

Available in March at your favorite retail outlet.

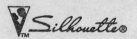 Silhouette®

HE'S MORE THAN A MAN,
HE'S ONE OF OUR

NANNY AND THE PROFESSOR
Donna Clayton

His son's new nanny taught Joshua Kingston a few things about child rearing. Now Joshua wanted to teach Cassie Simmons a few things about love. But could he persuade the elusive Cassie to be his wife?

Look for *Nanny and the Professor* by Donna Clayton, available in March.

Fall in love with our Fabulous Fathers!

Silhouette

R O M A N C E™

FF395

SAME TIME, NEXT YEAR
Debbie Macomber
(SE #937, February)

Midnight, New Year's Eve...a magical night with Summer Lawton that James Wilken knew could never be enough. So he'd spontaneously asked her to meet him again in exactly one year's time. Now that time had come...and with it, a friendly reunion that was quickly turning to love!

Don't miss
SAME TIME, NEXT YEAR,
by Debbie Macomber,
available in February!

She's friend, wife, mother—she's you! And beside each Special Woman stands a wonderfully *special* man. It's a celebration of our heroines— and the men who become part of their lives.

Don't miss **THAT SPECIAL WOMAN!** each month— from some of your special authors! Only from Silhouette Special Edition!

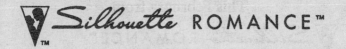

BELIEVING IN MIRACLES
by
Linda Varner

Carpenter Andy Fulbright and Honorine "Honey" Truman had all the criteria for a perfect marriage—they liked and respected each other, they desired and needed each other...and *neither* one loved the other! But with the help of some mistletoe and two young elves, these two might learn to believe in the miracle of Christmas....

BELIEVING IN MIRACLES is the second book in Linda Varner's MR. RIGHT, INC., a heartwarming series about three hardworking bachelors in the building trade who find love at first sight— construction site, that is!

Don't miss BELIEVING IN MIRACLES, available in December. And look for Book 3, WIFE MOST UNLIKELY, in March 1995. Read along as old friends make the difficult transition to lovers....

Only from *Silhouette*®

where passion lives.

This February from

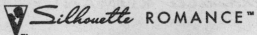

by
Carolyn Zane

When twin sisters switch identities, mischief, mayhem—and romance—are sure to follow!

UNWILLING WIFE
(FEB. '95 #1063)

Erica Brant agreed to take her sister's place as nanny for two rambunctious children. But she never considered that their handsome single father would want to make *her* his new bride!

WEEKEND WIFE
(MAY '95 #1082)

When a sexy stranger begged Emily Brant to pose as his wife for the weekend, it was an offer she couldn't resist. But what happens when she discovers he wants more than just a pretend marriage?

Don't miss the fun as the Brant sisters discover that trading places can lead to more than they'd ever imagined. SISTER SWITCH—only from Silhouette Romance!

SSD1

THIS SIDE OF HEAVEN

The miracle of love is waiting to be discovered
in Duncan, Oklahoma! Arlene James takes you there
in her miniseries, THIS SIDE OF HEAVEN.
Look for book four in February:

THE ROGUE WHO CAME TO STAY

Rodeo champ Griff Shaw had come home to Duncan to heal when he
found pretty single mom Joan Burton and her adorable daughter
living in his house! Griff wasn't about to turn Joan and her little girl
out, but did Joan dare share a roof with this rugged rogue?

Available in February, from

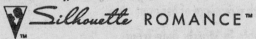

Silhouette ROMANCE™

WHERE **T**HE **H**EART **I**S

Don't miss the final book in
this heartwarming series from

ELIZABETH AUGUST

A HUSBAND FOR SARAH

Sam Raven had teased and challenged Sarah Orman as a girl, now he dared her to accept his wild proposal. Would Sarah's lifelong rival become her lifetime love?

WHERE THE HEART IS: With her wit and down-to-earth charm, Sarah Orman always had a way of bringing couples together. Now she finds a romance of her own!

Available in March, only from

Silhouette
R O M A N C E™